Maddie replaced
ing it with the typ
know if the pap
fraction of an i
eyes and caugh
mirror above Stacy's bureau. Gazing back at
her were the eyes of a thief, a cheat, and
Maddie turned away quickly.

"Sam would understand," she muttered defensively, feeling the color burn in her cheeks.
"She's always helping me out, covering for
me, saying that's what friends are for. If she
was here, she would say it's okay," she insisted.

In the middle of the room Maddie stopped
and shook her head emphatically. *I can't do
this*, she thought. *I can't do this to Sam.*

But it was too late. She didn't have any
other choice.

Other books in the **ROOMMATES** series:

COMING SOON

Roommates

MULTIPLE CHOICE
Alison Blair

BANTAM BOOKS
TORONTO · NEW YORK · LONDON · SYDNEY · AUCKLAND

MULTIPLE CHOICE

A BANTAM BOOK   0 553 17575 0

First publication in Great Britain

PRINTING HISTORY
Bantam edition published 1989

Bantam Books are published by Transworld Publishers Ltd.,
61–63 Uxbridge Road, Ealing, London W5 5SA,
in Australia by Transworld Publishers (Australia) Pty. Ltd.,
15–23 Helles Avenue, Moorebank, NSW 2170, and in New
Zealand by Transworld Publishers (N.Z.) Ltd., Cnr. Moselle
and Waipareira Avenues, Henderson, Auckland.

Printed and bound in Great Britain by
Hazell Watson & Viney Limited
Member of BPCC plc
Aylesbury, Bucks.

MULTIPLE CHOICE

Chapter 1

Madison Lerner looked down at her hands folded in her lap, then cast another quick glance at the door labeled Dean of Student Affairs. Any minute now, that door would open and the dean would say—

"Maddie, relax," came a reassuring voice from beside her. "He'll say it's okay, I know it."

With a grateful smile, Maddie met Samantha Hill's steady, warm gaze. Sam walked toward her, sat down next to her on the worn leather couch, and the two grinned at each other. "I know I'm acting like an idiot." Maddie sighed, shaking her head ruefully. "I just want to move in with you guys so much!"

"Well, don't worry. How can he say no? Terry moved out of the suite before spring break, so

1

we've had an empty bed for weeks." Sam swept back her wheat-colored hair and picked up an old course catalog that was sitting on the table next to her. Flipping through the pages, she added, "And nobody deserves to move in more than you do."

Maddie grimaced. "I just hope you're right." She looked at the closed door again and bit her lip. When she had transferred to Hawthorne College in the middle of her freshman year, there was no housing available, and she'd had to live off campus with her aunt. Unfortunately, one of the main reasons she had left Northwestern University was so she could get more involved in all the activities of a small campus. And living forty minutes away didn't give her much of a chance to do that.

So when Sam had invited her to move into her suite in Rogers House, which was right in the center of the pretty south quad, Maddie had jumped at the offer. Sam's suitemates, Stacy and Roni, had agreed wholeheartedly, so now it was just up to the dean. . . .

"What's taking so long?" Sam groaned, tossing the catalog back onto the table. Throwing a quick glance up at the wall clock, she shook her head. "You'd think it was some major policy decision or something."

"You don't have to stay," Maddie said hastily. She pulled at a lock of her dark wavy hair and looked anxiously into her friend's face. The dean had agreed to come in on Sunday morning to review the proposal, and Maddie felt she was putting everyone to a lot of trouble. She stood up and began pacing nervously. "I don't mind waiting by myself if you'd rather leave. I bet there's a ton of stuff you'd rather be doing."

"Oh come on, you know I don't mind waiting." Sam stood up and stretched. "Nothing could make me leave you here alone—as soon as that old coot comes out and gives us the good news, we're going to go out and celebrate!"

Behind them, someone cleared his throat. "Ahem. The 'old coot' has made up his mind."

Both girls whirled around, blushing to the roots of their hair. Dean Richardson was standing in the door of his office, a wry, amused look on his face.

"Uh, I—" Samantha stammered, and cast an imploring look at Maddie, who winced.

The dean held a file folder in his hands and tapped it gently against the door frame. "Miss Lerner," he said, speaking slowly. "After reviewing the situation, I have made a decision."

Maddie's heart sank. He was going to say no, she could tell. She closed her eyes.

"There are several other students who wish to change their housing, and you are by no means first on the list. But as your grades are excellent— you took five courses last semester and made dean's list, I see—and since you live off campus, I think it only fair to give you the opportunity. If you'll just fill out these forms, I think you can move into suite two C whenever you want."

Maddie's brilliant blue eyes flew open, and she stared first at the dean and then at Sam, her mouth opening in amazement.

"We did it!" shrieked Samantha, throwing her arms around Maddie.

"I can move in!" Maddie gasped, returning Sam's hug. "I can move in! I can't believe it!" She laughed and turned back to Dean Richardson. "Tell me what to fill in, and I'll do it!" she said.

"Maddie, this is so great," Sam whispered as Maddie bent over the dean's desk, pen in hand. "I can't wait to tell Stace and Roni."

Maddie nodded, hastily filling in the blanks in the housing forms. Ever since Samantha had first proposed the idea, down in Daytona Beach on spring break, Maddie had forced herself to remember that it was a long shot. Moving into a dorm after the middle of the semester was somewhat unusual, and there were all those other students ahead of her.

But now it had actually happened, and it was like a dream come true. It meant a complete change in Maddie's life. Instead of merely being on the outside of Hawthorne social life looking in, she'd be a part of it. She'd be able to join the clubs and organizations she'd read about, attend evening lectures and movies, or simply hang out in the snack bar over sodas and French fries, talking about nothing at all. Until now she'd felt left out, isolated—but that was all going to change now, thanks to Sam—and Dean Richardson.

"And you're sure your parents have agreed?" Dean Richardson asked as he sat down behind his desk and pulled the papers toward him.

"Yes, of course," Maddie answered quickly, not meeting his eyes. Her parents had agreed, but only after a long and heated debate. Both Mr. and Mrs. Lerner were professors at Northwestern University in Evanston, Illinois, where Maddie had studied until she decided to transfer. They knew better than most parents what kinds of distractions were commonplace on campus and warned Maddie that her grades were the most important aspect of her college experience, at least for now. And if they slipped at all, they'd have to reconsider.

Maddie was confident that she would have no trouble at all maintaining her straight A's, though. She'd been an ace student all her life, and just moving onto the campus wouldn't change that. The only thing that would change was her social life— and Maddie knew that could only get better!

She nodded again and met the dean's eyes. "They think it's a good idea," she said easily, and looked at Sam with a wide smile.

"Well then," Dean Richardson said with a short nod. He opened a drawer and extracted a set of keys. "Don't lose these," he warned Maddie sternly, handing her the keys. "The replacement fee is ten dollars. Welcome to Rogers House."

"You're kidding!" Roni screamed as she jumped up from the plaid couch. She bounded across the living room of suite 2C and enveloped Maddie in a big hug. "My new roomie!"

From a chair by the open window, Stacy Swanson smiled broadly. "That's great, Maddie." She rose gracefully and joined the others by the door. "I'm really glad you can move in here."

"I can hardly believe it," Maddie said, gazing around the suite with wondering eyes. She had seen it before when she'd visited—the slightly worse-for-wear furniture, the posters and stereo, the beautiful view from the balcony window. But she was seeing it now with new eyes, imagining where *her* posters would go. Biting her lip, she shook her head in amazement. "I guess I'll be moving in pretty soon."

"When?" Roni demanded, tossing her auburn hair over her shoulder. "Right now, right?"

Maddie raised her eyebrows and met Sam's look of encouragement. "Well, I—"

"It's all settled," Roni went on, confident as usual. She looked pointedly at Stacy. "You're driving, Swanson. We're moving this girl in."

Stacy raised her eyebrows slightly, then turned to Maddie. "I'd be glad to, ma'am," she said in a dignified tone. "Just let me get my keys."

"Well, actually," Maddie interrupted, "I drove over in my aunt's car."

The others looked at one another, and then Stacy nodded. "I know what. You drive back in your car, and Sam can follow you in my car to bring you back. And Roni and I will go get some treats to have for a celebration party. Okay?"

Maddie and Sam exchanged a smile, and then Sam let out a laugh. "Okay! What are we waiting for? Let's go."

An hour later, they had packed the trunk of Stacy's spacious Mercedes with Maddie's suitcases, boxes of books, knickknacks, and school supplies. Tossing her last bag of sweaters into the backseat, Maddie got in the car on the passenger's side and shut the door. "I can't even believe this is happening," she said dreamily as she settled back against the plush leather upholstery.

"Well, believe it." Sam laughed and put the car into reverse. She glanced at Maddie with a warm smile. "I'm really glad, Maddie."

"Me too. You know, I love my parents and everything, but it was really hard living at home last semester. They knew all my professors, and always wanted to know exactly what I was doing all the time in my classes." Maddie shook her head and gazed out at the telephone poles that lined the road. Going to the same university where her parents taught had made Maddie feel extremely confined. She couldn't enjoy the same freedom that all the other freshmen did. Moving in with her aunt here hadn't been much better. But that was all behind her now, she told herself happily. And she couldn't wait to be on her own for the first time.

"Mmm . . . that popcorn smells *so* good." Maddie curled her legs up underneath her on the couch and watched eagerly as the hot-air popper spewed out another batch of popcorn. She looked around her at the comfortable mess of suite 2C and already felt at home. Warm, late afternoon sunlight slanted in through the window, lighting Stacy's glossy blond hair where she sat framed by the curtains. All afternoon, Sam, Stacy, and Roni had helped Maddie unpack. Stacy had even lent her her favorite teddy bear to make her feel at home.

Sam leaned forward to adjust the bowl under the popper and smiled back at Maddie, her warm brown eyes glowing. "I'm really happy you could move in with us," she said. "It'll be so much fun having you here."

"Absolutely," Roni agreed as she reached up from the floor to grab a handful of buttery popcorn. "I was getting pretty lonely in my room there. And since Terry was our resident grind, it'll be good to have another live-in brain like you, Miss Never-Got-Below-an-A-in-Her-Life Lerner."

Rolling her eyes, Maddie unfolded her legs and propped them up on the coffee table. "I'm beginning to wonder if I was invited to move in here for some devious purpose," she teased.

"Whatever makes you think that?" Roni asked in an innocent voice, grinning disarmingly. "Oh! Time for a new record," she added, jumping up.

"Don't you touch my records with your greasy fingers," Stacy said, not even looking up from the magazine she was riffling through.

Roni rolled her eyes heavenward and grinned back at Maddie and Sam. "You know what we need?" she continued, placing the tone arm on a Genesis album. The strains of a lively dance tune pounded out of the speakers. "A raid!" she shouted above the music as she turned up the volume.

"Roni! Not another one!" Sam groaned, sliding down in the beat-up couch and covering her face with a pillow.

"Why? What kind of raid?" Maddie was alive with curiosity, and she looked eagerly from Sam to Roni and back again.

Sam peeked out from underneath the pillow and shook her head. "Roni's specialty is the shower raid—and believe me, she's good at it."

"But what is it?" Maddie prompted, a huge smile spreading over her face.

"Just come with me." Roni stood up and brushed an invisible speck of lint off her bright purple miniskirt. She crooked a finger at Maddie and grinned devilishly from under her long lashes. "You are about to be initiated into the fine art of shower raiding."

Jumping from the couch, Maddie followed Roni into their bathroom. "What do we do?"

Roni was rummaging in the cupboard under the sink for a cleaning bucket. "Just you watch," she said, turning on the cold-water tap in the tub and filling the plastic pail. "We can get another bucket from the utility closet down the hall for you."

A suspicion of what Roni was planning to do began to dawn in Maddie's mind, and she suppressed a shocked exclamation. "You aren't—"

Roni looked up with a gleam in her eyes as she twisted the tap off. "Oh, yes, I am! Come on." Bucket in hand, Roni trotted out through the suite and into the hall, with Maddie running behind her. "Lots of people take showers before dinner," Roni continued, pausing at one door. "Like Janet Fishbein, in here."

As Maddie watched, horrified, Roni opened the door of a nearby suite and poked her head in. The living room was empty, but from the bathroom came the unmistakable sound of a running shower. "Come on," Roni whispered.

She tiptoed across the living room and opened the bathroom door. A wave of steamy air hit them as they neared the shower, and the vague, shadowy figure of a girl was visible through the shower curtain. Drawing a deep breath, Roni dumped the contents of her bucket over the curtain rod, then dashed out of the room as the unlucky girl screamed.

"Oh, how could you!" Maddie laughed as she raced after Roni.

"Roni Davies! I know that was you!" the voice shrieked furiously.

"Come on!" Roni whispered, gesturing wildly to Maddie. They bolted back down the hall to their own suite and ducked inside the door, panting and giggling.

Across the room, Sam and Stacy shook their heads. "This means war, you know," Sam said with a wry smile.

"Do you think she'll tell on you?" Maddie gasped, meeting Roni's dancing eyes.

"Ha!" Roni scoffed with a sarcastic grimace. "She won't tell. There are better ways to get revenge, you know. So we'd better get ready for a counter-attack. Stacy, turn up the music, okay?"

With a chuckle, Stacy leaned across and turned up the volume, and the walls vibrated with the loud bass tones. Maddie couldn't believe this was happening—on her first day there!

"Let me do the next one," she said, taking the bucket from Roni's grip and heading for the bathroom.

Armed with a bucket full of icy water, Maddie and Roni stepped cautiously out into the hall again. "Suite two G," Roni mouthed. They tiptoed down the corridor to their next unknowing victim, and

Maddie opened the door with a trembling hand. Casting a quick glance over her shoulder at Roni, Maddie ran quietly across the room and dumped the bucket on another innocent shower taker. The screams were just as loud, and the two bandits ran breathlessly back to 2C and shut the door quickly.

"Any minute now," Roni gasped, leaning against the door. "Get some toilet paper."

Sam jumped up and ran to the bathroom, while Stacy slipped out onto the balcony, saying, "I'm not in this war! Do you hear me?"

A furious pounding on the door made Maddie jump, and she looked quickly at Roni, who was grinning with glee. "What do we do now?" Maddie whispered urgently. Her eyes darted around the room, and she wondered what weapon she should grab next.

Running back into the living room with two rolls of toilet paper, Sam nodded emphatically. "Okay. When I say when, open the door."

Roni nodded, and Sam pulled her arm back. *"When!"*

The door flew open, and Maddie had a brief glimpse of two girls wrapped in towels and armed with buckets. Sam flung the roll of paper out the door, and it sailed over the two girls' heads like a long streamer. Then the door slammed shut.

Pounding footsteps were heard in the hall, and Roni assumed the serious, ready-for-battle expression of an army general. "This is it, girls. Ready?"

Sam and Maddie nodded. "Ready," they replied in unison.

Screaming at the tops of their lungs, they dashed

out into the hall together, right into the middle of a full-fledged war. Maddie ducked as a roll of toilet paper whistled past her head, and she coughed and giggled as she inhaled a cloud of talcum powder. Everywhere she looked, girls were running back and forth, splashing each other with water and snapping towels at bare legs. For a moment she stood still, laughing uncontrollably as Sam was bombed with baby powder. It was a mistake. Suddenly, Maddie was drenched with cold water from behind. Gasping and spluttering, she felt the water drip down her back and into her eyes, and she wiped a hand across her face in astonishment. Across the hall, she met Sam's eyes—now Sam was laughing at her. She dimly heard someone trying to shout, "Cease fire!"

Everybody stopped running, and the shrieking subsided into gasping giggles. A short, redheaded upperclass girl walked down the hallway, shaking her head in dismay.

"It's Pam, our resident adviser," Sam whispered, moving over next to Maddie.

Pam stopped in front of Roni and folded her arms, trying to look stern. A floating scrap of toilet paper drifted down to land on her head, and a few muffled giggles escaped form the girls grouped behind her. Roni met Pam's eyes defiantly, and finally Pam burst out laughing.

"You are too much," she said, shaking her head in mock despair. "I hope when I come up here after dinner this hall will be clean enough for us to hold the president's reception," she added, raising one eyebrow at the group.

Roni saluted sharply. "Yes, ma'am."

Pam smiled and eyed Roni warily for a moment. Then she chuckled and turned to Maddie. "Hi. You must be the new girl in two C, right?"

Maddie nodded and wiped a drop of water off the tip of her nose as she felt the color rise to her cheeks.

"Hmm. I was told you were a dean's list student, four-oh average," Pam said, taking in Maddie's appearance with a speculative look. "But I guess Roni has an instant, devastating effect on everybody. Oh, well, another promising student bites the dust." Maddie laughed when she saw the twinkle in Pam's eyes. "Okay. I'd prefer to pretend this didn't happen." With that she turned on her heel and marched back down the hall and down the stairs.

"Okay, clean-up time! Come on," Roni commanded, taking her dripping suitemates by the arms. "All's fair in love and war."

Several hours later, Maddie climbed into her new bed and plumped up the pillows. Leaning on her elbow, she looked across the small bedroom at Roni, who was brushing her glossy auburn hair.

"I can't believe we did that." She chuckled and wiped a stray sprinkle of talcum powder off her ear.

"That? That was nothing," Roni said, her voice muffled as she bent over to brush her hair upside down. "Wait till we have a real war."

"I refuse to believe it can get worse than that." Maddie lay back and closed her eyes with a contented sigh. The whole day had passed so quickly it was almost a blur. It was hard to believe that just that morning she had been biting her nails outside the dean's office. And now she felt as though she'd been living in the dorm for the whole semester. So far it was everything she'd hoped it would be, and more: everyone was so spontaneous and ready to have fun. It was hard to imagine ever living *off* campus: missing all the excitement and the easy comaraderie of sharing a cozy suite. . . .

Maddie shook her head and hitched herself up on her elbow again. "You know, now that I'm on campus, I want to do everything. I've really missed not being able to get involved in all the things that go on after classes are over. I mean, half the reason I get such good grades is I never do anything *but* work. You know the old saying—all work and no play makes Maddie a dull girl. Smart, but dull."

Roni tossed her head back and scrambled across her bed to put her hairbrush on the nightstand. She gave Maddie a wry smile. "Just play it by ear, Maddie. Sure, there's a ton of stuff going on, but most of it's a real bore."

"Oh, come on! You just don't appreciate it, that's all," Maddie protested. "If you only knew how much I've wished I could join clubs and things, and just—just be *part* of everything."

Lying back on her pillows, Roni shrugged. "If you say so. Just don't go jumping into everything that happens. Take your time, see what's around. I can see how it must have been a drag living off campus, though," she admitted, turning her head to meet Maddie's eyes.

"It was." Maddie frowned thoughtfully, remem-

bering how frustrated she had felt. "I'll never forget that moment when Sam asked if I wanted to
live with you guys. God!" She laughed shortly. "I
would have done anything! She's such a nice person."

Roni smiled. "Yeah. Sam's a really good friend.
She'll do anything for the people she cares about."
Suddenly she grinned. "It's really great to have a
roommate again. I hated not having anyone to talk
to at night."

Maddie returned her smile, thinking that she had
never had anyone to talk to at night. But she was
already so wiped out that she let her new roommate do most of the talking. After what seemed
like only a few minutes, Maddie looked at the dig-
ital clock beside her bed.

"Oh, no! It's two o'clock in the morning!" she
gasped, meeting Roni's eyes in shock.

"So?" Roni stifled a huge yawn and settled down
farther in her covers. "We always stay up all
night—and sleep all day. That's just the way we
operate around here."

Maddie felt shocked—but pleased, too. Staying
up so late held a certain illicit attraction. She didn't
think she should do it *too* often, but it was part of
living in a dorm, and she was more than happy to
do it. As she switched off the light, Maddie felt a
sleepy smile spread over her face. Moving into
suite 2C was the best thing she'd ever done.

Chapter 2

"Maddie! Come on, wake up!"

With a sleepy groan, Maddie opened her eyes to see Sam's fresh face leaning over her. "Come on," Sam repeated, shaking Maddie's blanketed shoulder. "We'll miss breakfast."

Groggily pushing herself up into a sitting position, Maddie peered at the clock. It was ten minutes before eight.

"Oh, no," she muttered, rubbing her neck. Usually she woke up at seven, but at the moment she felt like she could sleep for another two hours—at least.

Sam yanked the covers off her and bustled around the room, pulling up the shades and opening Maddie's half of the big closet. "Come on, sleepyhead. We've got Shakespeare class in an hour."

"Don't remind me," Maddie said, stumbling out of bed. She looked stupidly around her, trying to think what she was supposed to do first. "Uh . . ."

"How late did you stay up last night, anyway?" Sam turned to her, holding out a rose-colored blouse and matching linen skirt for Maddie to put on, and raised her sandy eyebrows questioningly.

Maddie sent her friend a sheepish grin. "Two. We were just talking."

"I knew it! Roni will talk your ear off if you let her. Your challenge is don't let her take away your beauty sleep. Now come on, Maddie. Put this on."

Obediently, Maddie slipped into the outfit and pushed her feet into an old pair of scuffed blue flats. Shrugging into a light jacket, she followed Sam out into the living room. "Don't I even get to brush my teeth?" she complained. She squinted against the bright light streaming in the window.

"Nope. That's the penalty for oversleeping. Come on, let's get out of here."

Pausing only long enough to grab her notebook and shoulder bag, Maddie closed the suite door behind them. "Oh, I am so bushed," she grumbled as they stepped out into the clear morning. Overhead, a blazing blue sky was dotted with puffy light clouds, and under their feet the rust-colored Georgia clay was moist and soft. They crossed over the serene, glassy lake and entered the Commons for breakfast.

As they were sitting down at a table near the window, a tall, dark-haired boy joined them, kissing Sam lightly on the cheek.

"Hi, Aaron," Sam said, flushing with pleasure

under her freckles. She turned to Maddie with a shy smile. "Maddie this is Aaron Goldberg. Aaron, meet our new roommate Madison Lerner."

Quickly swallowing a mouthful of toast, Maddie reached out her hand to shake Aaron's. "Hi. It's nice to finally meet you," she said, wiping her mouth with a paper napkin. "I've heard a lot about you."

"And I've heard a lot about you," Aaron replied, straddling a chair. "I hear you're from Sam's hometown," he said. He helped himself to a sip of Sam's orange juice.

"Well, not exactly." Maddie grinned. "But I am from Illinois. I guess that's just about the same thing to people around here."

Sam scowled at Aaron. "He's from New York City, so he thinks of everything west of the Hudson River as a big desert."

With a hoot of laughter, Aaron nodded. "Well, that's pretty accurate, isn't it?"

"Not at all!" Maddie rejoined, pretending to be indignant. "Come on, Sam. Let's get out of here. We provincial types are always very early to class. It impresses the professors," she added for Aaron's benefit.

He grinned and stood up. "Okay, okay! I get the hint. See you later." He leaned down and kissed Sam again, then strolled away.

Glancing at her watch, Sam uttered a little cry of dismay. "You're not kidding. We're about to be late for class. It always takes forever to get through that stupid food line, let alone *eat*."

They hurriedly took their trays over to the conveyor belt, and as the remnants of their breakfasts sped away into the dark recesses of the enormous kitchen, the two girls ran out the door and down the broad marble steps. Within minutes they were walking up the shallow stairs of the big hall where the Shakespeare lectures were held.

It was a huge class, required for all English majors, and it was often hard to find two seats together if they got there late. In fact, it was because of Shakespeare class they had met, Maddie recalled as they politely edged their way down a row. When Samantha had seen her in the grocery store in Daytona Beach several weeks ago, she had recognized Maddie as a member of the big class.

As a friendly gesture, Sam had struck up a conversation, and when they found they were both from Illinois, they were soon exchanging hometown news like old friends. Maddie, in Daytona Beach with her parents, had instantly responded to Sam's outgoing, sympathetic nature, especially since she hadn't been able to make too many friends since her transfer to Hawthorne. By the time spring break was over, Maddie and Sam were close friends. Maddie glanced at Sam, feeling a rush of warmth and gratitude, and then looked down at her books with a shy smile.

Muffled whispers of a hundred voices filled the lecture hall, and Maddie opened her notebook to review her notes from the last class. Shakespeare was more than just a required course for her: her father's field of specialization was sixteenth- and seventeenth-century English literature, and that made it absolutely necessary for her to do well in the class. Suddenly a hush fell over the hall, and Maddie raised her eyes to look at the podium.

"Good morning," said Professor Harrison, Hawthorne's resident Shakespearean expert. He adjusted his glasses on the tip of his nose and experimentally tapped the microphone attached to the lectern. Peering over his lenses at the assembled students, Professor Harrison glanced briefly at his lecture notes and cleared his throat.

"Before we begin our discussion of *Antony and Cleopatra,* I would like to remind all of you that the, ah—" He consulted his notes briefly. "The *second* major paper for this class is due in three weeks' time. I'm sure you have all started by now," he added with heavy emphasis.

"Oh, I dread this paper," Sam whispered to Maddie. "I really want to do a good job."

"Me too," Maddie hissed back. "In fact, if I *don't* do a good job, I'll probably be disowned."

Sam giggled and lowered her head. "Well, you're probably almost done by now," she muttered through the side of her mouth.

"Not quite." Maddie grinned wryly. "No, all I did was write down some possible paper topics during break, and my Dad and I talked about it a lot, that's all."

"That's *'all,'*" repeated Sam with a teasing glare.

The professor's deep voice resumed. "And now, the topic of today's discussion of *Antony and Cleopatra* is the Bard's contrast between Rome and Egypt or, metaphorically, Virtue and Pleasure. This lecture could, in fact, be titled 'Love Versus the Demands of Empire.' As usual, please save any questions that you may have about my lecture for your section leaders."

Maddie's pen moved swiftly across the paper, her ears tuned sharply to the professor's voice. Even though she always did well in her classes, Maddie never let up on herself for a moment. She knew she fit right into the "grind" category, and she had taken a lot of teasing about it in high school. But education had always been her number-one priority. That was the way she had been raised, and she never questioned whether it was the right way to go or not. Her parents always assured her that it was.

"And now, to begin with, Cleopatra . . ."

"I can't believe I actually found you guys," Maddie said, putting down her tray and sliding into a chair next to Stacy. "This place is a madhouse at lunch." Across the table, Roni and Sam were poring over the campus newspaper.

Roni raised her eyes to Maddie's face and grinned. "That's because it's the one meal on the Hawthorne campus that almost everyone eats," she explained cynically. "At breakfast half the student body is still sound asleep, and at dinner the other half is out getting tacos or burgers in town."

"Well, it's pretty incredible if you ask me." Before now, Maddie had eaten her on-campus meals at the student snack bar—partly because it didn't make sense for her to buy a meal ticket and partly because she was too intimidated by the hoardes of students in the Commons. It was too overwhelming to walk in and sit down among so many total strangers. Besides, eating in the snack bar had given her more time to study. But now that she had her suitemates, she didn't have to worry about eating alone.

"Is that this week's newspaper?" she asked. She took a long drink of grapefruit juice and leaned forward across the table.

Samantha nodded and pushed it toward her. "There's nothing in it, as usual. Just scores from last week's games, announcements about upcoming dances."

"Bore bore bore," Roni intoned, making a long face.

"Well, there's a calendar of events, you know," Maddie reminded them, opening the paper to the middle. She ran her eyes quickly over the two-page spread, taking in the dozens of lectures, movies, debates, recitals, and productions. "I feel like I've been on a desert island for the past semester. I haven't been able to do a thing on campus, and now I want to do *everything.*" She chuckled at her own enthusiasm. "Well . . . almost everything." She met Sam's eyes with a grin.

"Well, don't spread yourself too thin," Sam cautioned her. "It's possible to devote every waking moment to extracurricular activities around here. Sometimes I wonder if the people who do all those things actually go to class."

Stacy looked at Sam with a bland expression in her wide eyes. "You mean—some people *do* go to class?" she asked in an awe-filled voice.

"Yes, can you believe it?" Roni asked, shaking her head in disgust.

"Come on, you guys," Maddie said, turning her attention back to the calendar of events. "I really mean it. There are so many interesting things going on all the time around here."

Stacy popped the last of her grilled-cheese sandwich into her mouth and wiped her fingers fastidiously with her napkin. "Well, if you want to do something really worthwhile," she said, pushing her chair back to face Maddie, "there's something going on tonight that you won't find listed on that calendar." She gave Maddie a grave, serious look.

"What? What is it?"

Sam reached across the table and gave Stacy a playful punch in the shoulder. "Stace, just because you think it's perfect for you doesn't mean she will." Turning to Maddie, Sam explained, "There's a sorority dinner tonight at APA—that's Alpha Pi Alpha—and Stacy wants to invite you to go with her."

With a stunned expression, Maddie looked at Stacy, who was grinning. "Are you serious? I didn't know you were in a sorority. Do you really want me to go with you?"

"Oh, please!" Roni groaned. "Listen, Maddie. It's not such a big deal Confidentially," she added, hiding her mouth with her hand and sending Stacy a mischievous look. "I think those things are Deadville."

"I don't believe it," Maddie insisted, frowning. She looked back at Stacy. "Is it a party? It must be fun to be part of a sorority—everyone being friends and everything."

Stacy giggled and put her hand on Maddie's arm.

"It's okay. It's just fun, that's all. It's nothing really special. Sam used to be a member, but she dropped out. I guess it didn't have enough glamour for her."

"Yeah, right!" snorted Samantha, who, Maddie noted, was the easygoing, girl-next-door type, not the glamorous type.

"Anyway," Stacy went on, ignoring Sam's and Roni's playfully exaggerated scorn. "APA is having a dinner party with the fraternity that we're sort of affiliated with, and I'd love it if you came with me. I could introduce you to a lot of people. And if you think it looks like something you want to get involved in, you can think about pledging. It's too late this year," she added with an apologetic smile, "but you can get a head start on next fall semester."

Maddie's head was swimming. "I can't believe it," she said. "It sounds great—I'd love to go!"

"Listen, you fascinating people," Roni cut in, getting to her feet. "I'm meeting Zack—we're taking a rowboat out on the lake. Pretty romantic, huh?"

Stacy stood up, too. "See you later," she said as she picked up her tray. "We should leave the dorm around six, so we'd better start getting ready around—"

"Three," interrupted Sam with an impish grin. She reached up and poked Stacy in the ribs, winking at Maddie. "This girl needs a lot of preparation time for a party."

"Say *five*," Stacy said severely, and then giggled. "See you later at the homestead."

"Bye," Maddie called as Stacy maneuvered her

way through the crowded dining hall. She stared
off into space as her friend disappeared, a blissful
smile on her face.

"Hey. Earth to Maddie," Sam called.

Maddie turned around with a guilty smile and
found Sam grinning at her. "I can't wait," she confessed.

Chuckling, Sam stood up and picked up her tray.
"I have to pick up some things at the bookstore.
Wanna come?"

Maddie took a final gulp of her juice and nodded
emphatically. "Definitely. I have to check out the
reading for some of the other English classes. So
far I haven't had time."

Sam shot her a humorous look. "Don't tell me
you plan to read books for courses you aren't even
talking."

"Well . . ." Maddie met her friend's eyes as they
dodged through the crowded room to drop off their
dishes. She shrugged. "They always look so interesting, I can't resist."

Sam rolled her eyes and tossed her empty milk
carton into a garbage can. "Give me a break, Lerner. Come on, let's go. And try to control yourself,
please." Chuckling, she headed for the stairs that
led to the basement bookstore. The girls put their
bookbags in lockers just inside the door and wan-
dered among the stacks.

"What are you getting, anyway?" Maddie called
over her shoulder as she stopped in the English
department section.

"Just a couple of notebooks."

Maddie nodded absently, her eyes running over

the stacks of books arranged by course title. Under a card labeled "Lord Byron and His Circle" she found the novel *Frankenstein* by Mary Shelley.

"Talk about a classic, huh?" Sam said as she came up beside her. "I was so surprised when I read that for the first time, weren't you?"

"Mmm. It's nothing like those stupid horror movies at all. I really loved it—it was so sad."

Sam reached for a book from a higher shelf. "I love this, too, don't you?"

Maddie read the title and gasped. "Are you kidding? *The Sun Also Rises* is one of my all-time favorites. Actually, anything by Hemingway is an all-time favorite." Biting her lip, she squatted down in front of a section of modern women poets and read the names aloud. "Sylvia Plath, Marianne Moore, Elizabeth Bishop—I love all of these." She stood up with a handful of slim paperbacks.

"You're not getting those, are you?" Sam teased.

Maddie shrugged. "Can I help it if I love to read?" she asked, her eyes twinkling. "And re-read?"

"Give me a break!" Sam laughed and took one of the books from Maddie, her expression suddenly thoughtful. "I've read these, too. You know," she mused, meeting Maddie's eyes with a warm smile, "I think we've probably read all the same books."

"I know—isn't it weird? I bet you've read every book I ever read."

Sam scoffed, arching one eyebrow as high as she could. "You've *got* to be kidding. You've read more books than anyone I know—half the writers you talk about I never even heard of."

"Oh, cut it out," Maddie muttered with a wry grin. She slid the books back on the shelf and linked her arm with Sam's, dragging her back down the aisle. "Listen, for the rest of the day, I'm not going to think about books at all. So let's get out of here—I've got to think about a party. Okay?"

"Okay!"

"What am I going to wear?" Maddie whined. She was standing in the middle of her room, wrapped in a fluffy terry towel. Drops of water were beaded on her shoulders, and her heavy dark hair clung damply to her neck.

She yanked hangers back and forth in the closet, sending her clothes swaying wildly. Nothing appealed to her—she didn't have anything appropriate for a sorority dinner party.

On her back on her bed, Roni scissored her legs above her in the air. "Sounds like you need a little 'wardrobe counseling,'" she said between little grunts of exertion. She swung her legs down and sprang up from the bed, coming to Maddie's side.

"Now let me see," she murmured, frowning into the closet. "No . . . not that. Maybe this . . ."

A frown creasing her forehead, Maddie watched as Roni examined her clothes. Suddenly Roni whirled around and took Maddie by the shoulders, peering into her face.

"We need to get the whole gang in on this, I think," she said seriously. "Stace! Sam! Get in here!" she hollered.

Maddie jumped at the sound of Roni's yelling, nearly losing her grip on her towel. Holding it close together, she turned as Stacy and Sam filed into the bedroom with curious smiles on their faces.

"This girl needs the professional treatment," Roni explained. She took a step backward so that she was standing next to the other two, and the three girls surveyed Maddie critically. "Vell, doctorz?" Roni asked in a heavy German accent. "Vat do you sink?"

"Hmm, ja." Sam rubbed her chin thoughtfully and walked in a circle around a grinning Maddie. "Dark haaaar. Pale skin—ze blue eyez. Delicate bone strrrructure. Ze subyect definitely needz mine blue dress!"

"Ja!" Stacy added, leaning forward to gaze analytically into Maddie's face. "Und—mine perrrrrlz. On zee vite skin—so lovely."

"Oh, I couldn't!" Maddie broke in at last, shaking her head and laughing at the same time. "You guys are lunatics, you know that?"

"Hey, don't knock it." Roni laughed, pulling Maddie into the living room toward Sam and Stacy's room. "Borrow clothes whenever you can—it's a cheap way to extend your own wardrobe."

Throwing open the closet, Sam pulled out a calf-length, royal-blue dress with a low-cut neck and full skirt. "I'm serious, Maddie. This would look so pretty on you. It's exactly the color of your eyes."

"And I have a pair of sandals the same color that Sam always wears with it," Stacy put in, rummaging in the pile of shoes at the bottom of the closet. A pair of strappy blue sandals appeared over Stacy's shoulder. "Like them?"

"Of course, but—" Maddie broke off, completely

bewildered. This "what's mine is yours and what's yours is mine" attitude was completely new to her. She had an older sister, but Marjorie was three inches taller and one size larger than she was. It was so wonderful to have friends to share things with that she couldn't stop smiling. "Thanks. They're perfect," she said finally.

"What are you going to wear?" she asked as Stacy fastened a string of lustrous pearls around her neck.

Stacy shrugged. "Oh, I don't know—some old rag, I guess."

Sam laughed heartily, and Maddie giggled. She already knew what kind of "old rags" Anastasia Vaughn Swanson had in her closet.

"You know," she said, grinning shyly at her suitemates, "I've never had so much fun. I'm so glad you asked me to live with you."

"Honestly, Maddie," Stacy muttered, zipping herself into a clingy dark gold dress. "I don't know how you ever got along without us."

Roni groaned. "Oh *please!*"

Maddie and Sam exchanged a look of amusement, and all four burst out laughing. "Well, I can tell you one thing," Maddie stated firmly as she leaned down to buckle the straps on her shoes, "I intend to enjoy living on campus, and I'm going to start the minute I get to APA."

With a last swipe of her blusher brush, Stacy turned from the mirror. "Let's get to it, then." She offered Maddie her arm. "Ready?"

Chapter 3

A calm and beautiful twilight was falling as Maddie and Stacy made their way across the landscaped campus, but Maddie was still so excited that she couldn't calm down. She couldn't believe everything was working out so well, so soon! Beside her, Stacy kept up a running commentary about the people they were about to meet.

"A lot of the guys are total jerks." Stacy laughed, pausing to extract a pebble that had worked its way into her sandal. "But not all of them, believe me. And most of them are really cute."

Maddie grinned as Stacy steadied herself on Maddie's arm. "That's nice to know," she said thoughtfully.

Darting her a quick look, Stacy said, "I guess

you haven't been able to date very much, huh?
Living forty minutes away and all."

"You're telling me!" Maddie shook her head, and
they continued down the gravel walk. "I don't
know—when you just see guys in class, it's hard to
get to know them."

"Well, your worries are over," her friend said,
waving to a pair of girls heading toward them from
the right. A steady stream of students was heading
for a large, Victorian house with a wide veranda,
and Stacy and Maddie headed up the broad steps.

"Is your boyfriend going to be here?" Maddie
asked.

"No, Pete doesn't really go for this kind of thing.
Here we are. Welcome to APA," Stacy said, gesturing broadly with her arm and giving Maddie a
wink.

"Hi, Stacy! Come on in!" A chorus of voices
greeted the two girls as they stepped into the
crowded front vestibule. Judging by Stacy's reception, Maddie guessed that she was a popular member of the sorority.

Within seconds Stacy was gabbing with a group
of girls at the bottom of the staircase, and she put
her hand on Maddie's arm, pulling her forward.
"Everybody, this is my new suitemate, Maddie Lerner," she said with an enthusiastic smile. "Maddie,
this is everybody!"

Laughing, Maddie nodded at the smiling girls
facing her. "Hi, everybody."

A tall fair girl stepped forward to shake her
hand. "Welcome to Alpha Pi Alpha, Maddie. I'm

Helen Armstrong, and this is Sandra Tapp, Holly Dieter, and Ginny Johnson."

Maddie smiled at each girl in turn and turned to Stacy as her friend took her by the arm again. "Come on, I want to show you around."

"Nice to meet you!" Maddie called over her shoulder to the group by the stairs. "This is a really pretty house," she added as Stacy led her through the living room and into a dining room crowded with people.

"Some of the upperclassmen in the sorority live here," Stacy explained over the clamor of voices, leading Maddie to a buffet table. "I was thinking about moving here, but since Sam dropped out, I don't know. Wow, look at all this food."

The buffet table was laden with an enormous array of cheeses and fruit, steaming dishes of lasagna, and a variety of salads. At the far end, pitchers of juice and bottles of soda stood in a jumbled mess on the damp tablecloth. To her surprise, Maddie also noticed some boys standing by the window drinking cans of beer.

"Is that allowed?" she asked, nodding her head toward them.

"Is what allowed? Oh!" Stacy rolled her eyes and popped a grape into her mouth. "A lot of people drink, even though they're mostly underage. Officially, there's no alcohol served here, but somehow, someone always brings it. That's just part of college. I don't think it'll ever change."

Maddie nodded thoughtfully and wondered if she would be offered an alcoholic drink. She met Stacy's eyes again and shrugged.

"Oh, there are some friends of mine I want you to meet," Stacy said. "Come on."

Grabbing a sliver of cheese, Maddie followed obediently, and they headed for a group of boys near a big bay window. Evidently they all knew Stacy because they all turned to greet her as the two girls walked up.

"Hi, guys," Stacy said with a brilliant smile. "I want you all to meet my new suitemate, Maddie, and I want you all to be especially nice to her," she added flirtatiously. "I'll be right back."

Maddie felt herself blushing as the five boys turned their attention to her. She was immediately surrounded and responded shyly to their greetings.

"I'm Dan Dreyfus," said a tall, good-looking boy with penetrating brown eyes. He spoke as if she should already know who he was. "Can I get you something to drink?"

"Um, some Seven-Up or something like that," she said, chickening out of having a drink at the last minute. She didn't want to make a bad first impression at this place—she'd never be asked back. "Thanks."

As she turned to watch Dan go over to the buffet, she noticed a boy on the outskirts of the group who was smiling at her. "I know you!" she cried with a feeling of relief at seeing a familiar face. "You're in my classical Greece class, aren't you? You sit in the back, right?"

He nodded, then shook his sandy blond hair off his forehead. "I'm Stu Peterson," he said, the corners of his green eyes crinkling. "What do you think of that Dr. Bianci, huh? A real bore."

Suppressing a giggle, Maddie nodded. "I—"

"Here's your Seven-Up," Dan interrupted, coming up beside her.

"Oh—thank you." Flustered, Maddie took the cup he held out. Then she turned back to Stu, wondering if she could talk to both of them at once.

Ignoring Stu, Dan hitched himself up on the windowsill and crossed his arms. "So, did you just transfer to Hawthorne?" he asked, looking at her intently. "Isn't it kind of late in the year?"

"Oh, well, actually I transferred at the beginning of the semester, but I only moved in with Stacy this past weekend." Maddie turned her head just in time to see Stu walking off, and she felt a pang of disappointment.

"So we should see more of you, then. Stacy . . ."

"Did I hear my name?" Arching her fair eyebrows, Stacy joined them by the window and looked reproachfully at Dan. "Listen, Dan. Don't try to monopolize Maddie. There are a million people I want to introduce her to!" she chided playfully.

"Hey, I was just trying to be polite," he said, holding out his arms in gesture of wounded innocence. But the meaningful twinkle in his dark eyes suggested something else as he looked back at Maddie again. "I'll see you later, I hope."

Stacy led Maddie away, and under her breath, she said, "He is notorious, Maddie. He's tried to get every girl in this school into bed, and he's very persistent."

Shocked, Maddie stared at her friend, then craned her neck to look back at Dan Dreyfus. He was already deep in conversation with another girl. "Geez," she whispered, swallowing hard. "I had no idea."

With a light chuckle, Stacy shook her head and looked fondly into Maddie's eyes. "No, I guess you didn't. Anyway, come on into the library. That's where I always hang out during a party."

Maddie followed Stacy into a small, book-lined room, where another, smaller buffet was set up. It was a cheerful, comfortable-looking study, and Maddie recognized Holly Dieter sitting on one of the overstuffed sofas.

"Hi," Holly called out, waving them over.

"I'll go get us something to eat," Stacy said, giving Maddie a gentle push. "Sit down, make yourself at home."

Smiling gratefully, Maddie crossed the room and sat down next to Holly with a sigh. "This is a really pretty room," she said, looking around at the framed prints on the walls and the glowing, shaded lamps.

"Yeah, it's the best place during a party, because it's quiet. But sooner or later, everyone ends up coming in here. So you get to see everybody, but you don't get crushed." Holly crossed her long legs and turned on the couch to face Maddie. "So, how long have you known Stacy?"

"Only a few weeks," Maddie admitted, reaching for a dish of nuts on the table in front of them. She tossed a Brazil.nut into her mouth and smiled affectionately. "We met over spring break in Daytona. But she's really great. I like her a lot—and Sam and Roni, too. Do you know them?"

"Sam I know," Holly said, tucking a blond curl behind one ear. "And sooner or later, everyone on campus runs into Roni Davies!"

The two girls chuckled. Maddie was glad that she had come. For some reason, it seemed perfect to be sitting in this cozy room with the tantalizing hum of a busy party on the other side of the door and talking with Holly.

"I know what you mean," Maddie said with a sigh. "Roni seems to be everywhere at once. Which is something I wish I could do," she confessed, meeting Holly's inquisitive gaze. "When I lived off campus, I felt so out of it all the time. I'd really like to get more involved at Hawthorne."

Holly leaned forward and put her hand on Maddie's arm. "Listen, I know the perfect way for you to do that."

"What's that?" Stacy asked, sitting gracefully on the edge of the coffee table and handing Maddie a plate of lasagna and salad.

"Thanks, Stace. Yes, what?" Maddie added, turning back to Holly as she carefully raised a fork-ful of the steaming pasta to her mouth.

"Well, I belong to a group called the Gold Key Guides—have you ever heard of it?"

Maddie shook her head.

Holly turned herself a little more toward Maddie on the couch and laid her arm across the back. "They take college applicants—usually high school seniors—and incoming freshmen on tours of the campus with their parents. You know, show them around, give them a sense of what goes on here at Hawthorne. I've done a lot of tours, and you'd be surprised how much more I know about the school than I used to."

Swallowing another bite of lasagna quickly, Maddie nodded. "That sounds like a great idea. How do you get in?"

"You have to have perfect grades," Stacy added. "But of course *you* qualify."

Maddie looked from Stacy to Holly and back again. "Is that the only requirement?"

"Well, you have to be pretty familiar with the campus, and be friendly and outgoing and stuff, but I'm sure you can get in with no trouble," Holly assured her. "Listen, all you have to do is study a campus map, read the calendar, just be aware of the things that are going on so you can talk about it like an old pro. And you only have to do as many tours as you want."

Thinking carefully, Maddie pushed her fork around on her plate as she considered Holly's suggestion. It sounded like the perfect way to find out everything about Hawthorne, and Holly was so enthusiastic about it. Maddie was positive the Gold Key Guides was the club she had been looking for.

"Is there some kind of interview or something?" Stacy asked, scraping together the last bits of lettuce on her paper plate. She grinned at Maddie. "I get the feeling you're interested, Miss Lerner."

"I am," Maddie agreed. She turned to Holly. "What do I have to do?"

Holly laughed. "There's a meeting tomorrow at ten-fifteen in Wagner, room one twelve. Do you think you can make it?"

"Definitely!"

"Good." Holly pushed herself up off the couch and smiled down at them. "I have to see what's going on in the kitchen," she said, rolling her eyes. "With the guys helping out, it can turn into a real disaster zone. So I'll see you tomorrow, okay?"

"Sure. See you later!" Maddie watched as the tall girl crossed the room and slipped out the door, and then she turned to Stacy with a grin. "I can't believe it—it sounds perfect!"

Stacy laughed and drained the rest of her club soda. "If that's your cup of tea, be my guest," she said wryly. "Personally, I can't see ushering a bunch of high school kids around by *choice*. But if you want to . . ."

"I do. I really do." Maddie leaned back against the couch, lost in thought. Joining the Gold Key Guides could turn out to be the best way to get what she wanted—the total picture of campus life. And she was determined to make a success out of it. She looked up as Stacy got to her feet. "Are you leaving?"

"Just for a few minutes—I should really help out in the kitchen," Stacy said with a grimace. "Do you mind if I leave you here by yourself for a while?"

Maddie faked an expression of sheer terror. "Well," she said in a quavery voice, "I—I guess I'll be okay. But hurry back!"

With a lopsided grin, Stacy leaned over and lightly slapped Maddie's knee. "Chicken."

Maddie giggled and waved Stacy away. "Go on, I don't mind at all. I'll just stay here and stuff myself on this incredible lasagna."

"Good. See you later."

Once Stacy was gone, Maddie turned her attention to dinner. She was daydreaming about how popular she'd be around campus in a few months when someone sat down next to her. Startled, she looked up quickly. Stu Peterson was smiling back at her.

"Hi," she said, feeling herself blush slightly. "Sorry we got interrupted before."

"No problem." His eyes twinkled as he added. "Dan Dreyfus has a tendency not to notice anyone but pretty girls."

Maddie looked back down at her plate, then glanced back hesitantly at Stu from the corner of her eye. He was grinning at her so openly that she had to smile back.

"So, what brings you to this soirée?" Stu said, politely taking her empty plate and putting it on the table. "Were you dying of curiosity to see what goes on inside the infamous APA house?"

"Well, sort of," Maddie said with a light laugh. "But actually, I just moved onto campus—I share a suite with Stacy—and she invited me to come with her tonight."

He nodded and rubbed his chin thoughtfully for a moment. "So, what's the verdict?"

"The verdict?"

"Is this everything you expected it to be?" he asked with a wry grin.

Maddie met his eyes evenly, then burst into giggles. "I'm not sure. To tell you the truth, I guess I was expecting a lot of sophisticated preppies talking about polo games and trips to Paris. Dumb, huh?"

"The truth is," Stu said with an ominous frown, "people in sororities and fraternities are no different from anybody else. They just think they are. So they formed into bunches and gave themselves Greek names."

Maddie chuckled. "I guess you're right. Speaking of Greek, why are you taking the classical Greece course? Are you majoring in history?"

Looking quickly behind him, Stu leaned forward and whispered conspiratorially. "I'll tell you a secret."

Maddie's eyes danced as she whispered back, "What is it?"

"I'm a classics major. But please don't tell anyone else."

With a peal of laughter, Maddie sat back and looked into Stu's twinkling green eyes. "Now what's so horrible about that?"

"Well, it's not exactly going to get me a cushy job on Wall Street," he said, looking sheepishly at his glass of soda. "My parents just can't understand why I want to major in something as 'useless' as classics."

Maddie shook her head emphatically. "Listen, my parents for one would love to see more classics majors. They're both professors, so the scholarly, useless majors are their favorites."

"No kidding? Where do they teach?" Stu leaned back and put his arm along the back of the couch, tilting his head to one side as he looked attentively at her.

"Northwestern—it's near Chicago."

He nodded. "Pretty impressive. How come you

didn't want to go there? Or is that a stupid question?"

"It's not so stupid," Maddie said, smiling. "Actually, I started out there. But I found it was much too big for me—I felt like a little atom in a huge universe. Know what I mean?"

"Yeah. Then Hawthorne is a pretty drastic change, isn't it?" He grinned at Maddie.

She laughed back. "You can say that again!" For a moment, they just looked into each other's eyes, not saying anything, and Maddie felt her heart flutter with excitement. It was great to meet a guy who was so warm and nice—so far, *two* great things had come out of this party.

"So . . . how about seeing a movie sometime?" Stu finally broke the silence. "Do you like old movies?"

"Sure. As long as they're *classics,*" she teased.

He touched her shoulder lightly. "Great. I'll call you—and here comes your chaperone, I see," he added as Stacy walked up to them with a curious look in her eyes.

"Hi, Maddie. Ready to go?" Stacy looked from Maddie to Stu and back again. "Or did I pick a bad time to come back?"

With a glance at her watch, Maddie exclaimed, "Oh, no! Not at all. It's pretty late—I mean, I've got an early class tomorrow." She stood up slowly, smoothed her skirt, and smiled at Stu. "See you in class?"

"Sure will. Nice to meet you, Maddie."

As they walked down the veranda steps, Stacy

linked her arm with Maddie's and squeezed it. "You were a big hit, you know."

"Was I really?" Maddie stopped and looked back at the brilliantly lit house they had left behind. She smiled at Stacy in the darkness, then hugged her spontaneously. "Thanks so much for inviting me Stace. I had a really great time."

"So I could see!"

"Mmm." Maddie sighed and tilted her head back to look at the stars as they walked slowly toward Rogers House. "What a wonderful night."

Stacy chuckled and reached into her purse for her door keys. Climbing the stairs to the second floor behind her friend, Maddie felt a pleasant weariness steal over her. So far, living on campus was turning out to be fantastic.

"Hi, you guys, how did it go?" Sam called out as they opened the door of suite 2C.

Kicking off her shoes, Stacy flopped down on the plaid couch and smiled impishly at Maddie. "Well, within about two minutes of getting there, she had Dan Dreyfus panting over her."

Sam gasped and closed her book with a snap. "You're kidding!" She stared at Maddie in amazement and shook her head. "You don't waste any time."

Before Maddie could protest, Stacy cut her off. "But I took care of that, don't worry." She gave Maddie another arch smile before turning to Sam again. "And she made another conquest, too."

"Oh, cut it out," Maddie said, blushing furiously as she sat down in the chair by the window. But she couldn't help smiling as she remembered her long conversation with Stu Peterson and the tingle of excitment she felt when they had looked into each other's eyes.

"Well, who is it?" Sam demanded sternly. "Come on, spit it out."

"It's not such a big deal!" Maddie insisted weakly. She looked helplessly from Stacy's grinning face to Sam's and blushed again. "A guy named Stu Peterson—and we just *talked,* that's all."

Stacy smiled wryly and put her hand on Sam's arm. "Confidentially, Sam, don't listen to her. Does the expression 'stars in their eyes' mean anything to you?"

"Stacy! It wasn't *that* big a deal."

"But you forget that I *saw* you two!" Stacy said breezily, and then tossed a pillow at Maddie. "And anyway, so what? He's a really nice guy. It's nothing to be ashamed about."

Maddie stood up, trying to maintain a calm expression. But it was almost impossible to keep from smiling. "I don't have to stay here and take this abuse," she said regally. *"I'm* going to bed."

Laughing, Sam waved good night. "Okay, Cleopatra. Sweet dreams." Stacy and Sam burst into laughter, and Maddie stuck out her tongue at them and walked into her bedroom.

As she closed the door behind her, Maddie let her shoulders relax. The party had been wonderful, and she had made several new friends—best of all, Stu and Holly. She stepped out of her shoes and unzipped Sam's royal-blue dress, hung it up carefully, and then threw on her nightgown.

Tomorrow she would go to the Gold Key Guides

meeting, and on Wednesday her classical Greek history class met. Blissfully, Maddie wiggled her toes as she stretched her legs out under the covers. And the moment she put her head on the pillow, she was fast asleep.

Chapter 4

A deafening clamor jolted Maddie awake, and she sat up in bed, her heart hammering wildly. "What is it?" she gasped, turning terrified eyes to Roni in the semidarkness.

Roni switched on the light. "Relax—it's just a fire drill," she shouted above the noise. "Grab your pillow—come on."

Trembling with the adrenaline that was coursing through her veins, Maddie threw on her bathrobe and picked up her pillow to stumble after Roni into the living room. Stacy and Sam were just coming out of their own bedroom, looking bleary-eyed and irritated as they pulled on their own robes over their nightgowns.

"Why do fire drills always have to be at two in the morning?" Sam groaned, yanking open the suite door. The four girls filed out into the hallway, already crowded with girls in pajamas running for the stairs. "Come on."

They left the door open behind them and joined the throng in the corridor. Now that she knew it was only a drill, Maddie's panic had subsided, and she began to look on it as an adventure. Within seconds they were all down in the front lobby of Rogers House, where everyone else was grumbling and milling around.

"All right! All right!" Pam shouted above the noise. Suddenly the deafening fire alarm was switched off, and the silence was a tremendous relief. Scrambling up onto a chair, Pam grinned mischievously at everyone.

"Yes, it's another fire drill, ladies. And since you were all twenty seconds over the allowed time at the last one, we'll have to have at least one more before the semester's over." A chorus of protests rose up, and Pam waved her hands for silence. "But," she continued, consulting a stopwatch in her hand. "We made it this time. Forty-five seconds!"

All the girls roared in triumph, and some people clapped. Maddie couldn't believe it had all happened in less than a minute. She grinned at Sam, who pushed her mussed-up blond hair out of her eyes and gave Maddie a sleepy, lopsided smile.

Pam called loudly for attention. "Did we start at the end of the alphabet last time or at the beginning?"

Instantly there were conflicting yells of "End!" and "Beginning!" and "Start in the middle for a change!" Shrugging, Pam consulted her list. "I think I'll go by suite."

As Pam began reeling off names, the girls called out "Here!" and many of them plodded wearily back upstairs as soon as they had been accounted for. Several names were answered with silence, until someone called "She's out!" and muffled giggles rippled through the crowd in the lobby.

"Where would someone be at two in the morning?" Maddie whispered to Sam, working her feet more securely into her slippers.

"At a party? Or . . . out with a friend?" Sam suggested innocently.

Confused, Maddie looked at Sam and then noticed a couple of boys standing awkwardly at the edge of the crowd. Suddenly she realized what her friend was getting at. She could tell her normally pale skin was now a bright shade of pink. "You mean —?"

"Maddie, for heaven's sake, don't look so scandalized!" Roni muttered, stifling a yawn. "We're lucky if half the residents of Rogers House are here for a fire drill."

"Suite two C!" Pam called. "Roni, Samantha, Stacy, Maddie!"

"Unfortunately we're all here," Roni snarled, giving Pam a fierce look that made the resident adviser burst into laughter.

"Oh, you poor things," Pam crooned, making four little marks on her list.

"Well, I don't know about you guys," Sam said, yawning and covering her gaping mouth with one hand. She stretched and rolled her neck with a groan. "But I for one am not waiting for dough-nuts." With that announcement she turned and padded toward the stairs in her slippers.

Maddie watched her leave with a puzzled frown. "What did she mean, doughnuts?" she asked Roni.

"It's our reward for making the fire drill," Stacy explained, turning back after talking to a next-door neighbor. "If you feel like it, there will be dough-nuts and hot chocolate in the living room in a few minutes. For being such good girls," she added as she rolled her eyes.

"Are you going?" Maddie asked.

Stacy shook her head as though the very idea were absolutely inconceivable, and Roni chuckled. "Nah—not me, I'm on a diet tonight."

Looking from Stacy to Roni and back again, Maddie felt torn with indecision. Apparently, the cool thing to do was act as though the middle-of-the-night treat were no big deal. But to Maddie, it sounded like fun. Just then Pam jumped down from her perch and waved at the girls still standing there.

"Okay, kiddies. Time for dinner!"

"Are you staying up?" Roni asked Maddie, turning to head back up the stairs.

"Well . . ." Maddie watched longingly as two dozen or so girls filed into the living room, then turned back to her roommate. "Just for a few min-utes, I guess. I'm a little hungry."

Roni shrugged and let out another gigantic yawn. "Okay, see you later."

"Come on, baby bear." Stacy sighed and draped her arm across Roni's shoulders. "Time for beddy-bye. See you tomorrow, Maddie," she called with a tired smile.

"Sure. Sleep well, you guys!" Wrapping her bathrobe tighter around her, Maddie smiled and then walked into the living room.

"Hi, Maddie," a voice called out. "Come on and join the party!" It was Laura Malone from the fourth floor, a freshman who was infamous for her rowdiness. As Maddie crossed the room to investigate the box of doughnuts, somebody turned on the radio, and music began beating out of the speakers.

"Okay!" Laura laughed, jumping to her feet with a doughnut in her hand. "Let's dance!"

Without an instant's hesitation, everyone began to dance around the living room, and Maddie found herself being bumped into and whirled across and around the room. Wherever she looked, girls in every type of nightwear—from lacy negligees to New York Mets T-shirts—were laughing and moving around to the music. Giggling self-consciously, Maddie jumped onto a chair and pumped her arms like a sixties go-go dancer. The music was turned up, and Maddie heard someone yell, "Let's order some pizzas!"

Pam shook her head and shrugged in defeat. "Don't stay up too late, you guys! And don't be *too* loud!" she warned. She ducked out of the room with a shriek as someone playfully threw a slipper at her.

Breathless with laughter, Maddie smiled at Jenny Forester, who was dancing on the couch next to her, as the music switched from the Rolling

Stones to Bruce Springsteen. A general whoop of excitement went up as the Boss began to sing, and Maddie pushed her hair out of her face. She'd never seen a party break out so quickly—and get into such a high gear so fast. She loved it!

"This is great!" she yelled at Jenny, who was using a glazed cruller as a microphone while lip-synching the lyrics. Jenny grinned back at her and nodded.

Fifteen minutes later there was another yell of triumph as a bleary-eyed delivery man brought in five steaming pizza cartons. Someone dashed upstairs for money, and the girls fell on the pizzas like a pack of hungry wolves. As Maddie pulled a gooey string of mozzarella cheese off a slice, she sighed with satisfaction.

Somewhere in the back of her mind she knew it must be at least three o'clock in the morning, but she couldn't bring herself to leave the party, as tired as she was. It was too much fun. She looked around and sat down on the edge of a coffee table. This was exactly what she had moved onto campus for, and she wasn't about to miss it!

"I hate to say this, but you look like death warmed over."

Maddie tried unsuccessfully to restrain a jaw-breaking yawn and sent Samantha a jaundiced look across the breakfast table. "Hmm . . . thanks. That's more or less how I feel." Yawning again, she pushed her spoon cautiously around in her bowl of cornflakes, then shoved it away. "Actually, I think that fourth slice of pizza is still with me," she moaned feebly, feeling more than slightly nauseated.

"Listen, you guys," Roni said, throwing herself into a chair next to Sam. "Help me out here—I'm desperate. I've got to come up with some statistics for my psych presentation about how ambition is related to diet."

Sam raised her eyebrows skeptically. "Did you do a survey or something?"

"Well, I was going to," Roni admitted frankly, helping herself to Maddie's abandoned cornflakes. Her auburn curls bobbed as she shook her head and added, "But I sort of never got around to it."

Maddie didn't want to let Roni see how shocked she was, but she couldn't help it. "You mean, you're going to fake the results—make up some statistics?" She tried to keep herself from sounding *too* appalled.

Shrugging, Roni made a clicking noise with her tongue. "Yeah, I guess so. I mean, I asked *some* people, though," she continued hastily as though sensing Maddie's discomfort. "Just not enough to make accurate stats."

Sam and Maddie exchanged a glance across the table, and Sam shrugged. Maddie looked down at her tray, and Roni slumped forward to rest her arms on the table.

"Well, we've got to get to class," Sam said, picking up her empty dishes. "All I can tell you is that my main ambition right now is to get to Shakespeare on time."

"Okay, see you at lunch," Roni said, sitting up

and pulling her psych notebook out of her bag with a scowl. "I'll think of something."

Maddie was silent all the way to Shakespeare, partly out of fatigue and partly out of preoccupation. There was no question in her mind that in spite of everything, Roni was a good student and did care about her grades. But it was so hard to believe that she was going to ... well, cheat. And that her suitemates didn't care if she did!

She followed Sam down the steps in the lecture hall and wearily lifted her big Riverside Shakespeare book up onto the writing arm of her chair. Professor Harrison strode across the podium, exuding his usual aura of lofty intellectualism. Without delay, he began his second lecture on *Anthony and Cleopatra*, using a slide presentation to demonstrate some of the historical and geographical references about ancient Rome and Egypt.

Maddie shook her head groggily, trying to concentrate as the slides swam in front of her eyes. But it was no use: the hall was warm, and the lights were dim. The fold-down seats were even comfortable. Without much of a struggle against sleep, Maddie dozed off. The professor's voice faded to a vague, droning hum as a kaleidoscope of images flashed before Maddie's closed eyes. She saw the faces of her suitemates dancing in slow motion around the Commons and herself ushering a crowd of wide-eyed high school students to a table covered with pepperoni pizzas. "You'll love living on campus," she told them solemnly, handing out slices of pizza to their parents. Roni flitted around the room, asking everyone what they wanted to do after they finished breakfast, and Sam came up to Maddie and poked her in the ribs.

"Maddie!"

With a jolt, Maddie sat up, momentarily disoriented. She was in Shakespeare class. Next to her, Sam was smiling sympathetically. "You fell asleep, you idiot."

Drawing a deep breath, Maddie nodded. She had no idea how long she'd been asleep, and an unpleasant sensation of guilt swept over her. She had never fallen asleep during a class before, and the only reason she had done it now was because she had been staying up too late, having fun.

"Don't worry," Sam whispered, writing quickly as the professor talked. "You can borrow my notes later to see what you missed."

"You wouldn't mind?"

"Of course not! That's what friends are for, you dummy."

Relief and gratitude replaced Maddie's guilt, and she smiled warmly at her friend. "Thanks a lot. You're a real pal."

Sam grinned back. "I know, I know. Now be quiet, okay? But not *too* quiet," she teased.

With a firm resolve to take down every word Professor Harrison said, Maddie focused her attention on him for the rest of the class. And in the back of her mind she gave herself a stern scolding, vowing never to fall asleep in class again.

Finally, the professor brought the lecture to a close, and he took off his glasses to rub his eyes. Then he drew his bristly eyebrows together and leaned forward on the lectern. "I would like to take this opportunity to announce that the English department is putting together a production of *A Midsummer Night's Dream* in the next few weeks," he said succinctly. "And although we are not covering this play during the semester, I strongly urge you to see it—on the off chance that there will be a question about it on the final exam."

A series of muffled groans rippled through the auditorium, and as the professor left the podium, the students all began to talk at once. Amid the bustle of seats being set upright and papers being shuffled together, Sam and Maddie gathered their books and stood to join the slowly moving mass of bodies walking up the aisle.

"I guess we're seeing *A Midsummer Night's Dream*, then," Sam said wryly as they moved up the steps.

Maddie shook her head swiftly. She had a much better idea. "Not me."

"What do you mean? You heard what Harrison said."

With an arch look, Maddie glanced at her friend. "I'm not going to *see* the play. I'm going to be *in* it."

"Oh, great! Now I've heard everything!" Chuckling, Sam caught the heavy door as it swung back at her and pushed it open again. "I didn't know you were a stellar actress on top of everything else."

Maddie grinned as they stepped outside into the sunlight. Squinting, Sam hoisted her heavy books onto one hip and pressed her lips together with a thoughtful frown. "So listen," she said, tipping her head to one side. "I know you're probably so far ahead you don't need to do any work on your paper, but do you want to hit the library with me now? I have to do some of the reserved reading, and then get a start on this monster of a Shakespeare paper."

'Hmm." Maddie caught her lower lip between her teeth and hitched up her sleeve to glance at her watch. "Oh, wait a second," she gasped, slapping her forehead with her free hand. "I almost forgot!"

"What?"

"I didn't tell you last night, but I met a girl at the APA party—Holly Dieter?"

Sam nodded. "Sure, I know Holly."

Maddie swept her dark hair back over her shoulder. "Well, she asked if I wanted to go to a meeting today for the Gold Key Guides, and it's in ten minutes. It's across campus, so I've really gotta run."

"You're going to join Gold Key?" asked Sam, lifting her eyebrows slightly and readjusting her bag over her arm. "Isn't that some kind of tour guide thing?"

Maddie nodded. "Yeah. I think it sounds like fun—and a great way to get into campus activities. So I'll see you later, okay?"

"Sure. See you at lunch."

As Sam turned to head for the library, Maddie watched her for a moment with a fond smile on her face. Studying with Sam would have been fun, and she needed to tackle *her* paper, too. But for the moment, she was just too busy: she had to go to the Gold Key meeting, then lunch and calculus, pick up a copy of the play, and meet with her faculty adviser. Then there would be dinner, and she and Jenny Forester had made a date to watch an old movie playing at the campus cinema. By the time she hit home base again, it would be about time for bed—after a little reading, of course. So for that day, at least, William Shakespeare and Professor Harrison were going to have to wait. Maddie wanted to do a good job on her paper, but there was still a lot of time left. Right now making friends was more important. Wasn't that what freshman year was all about?

Chapter 5

When Maddie pushed open the swinging door of room 112, she found herself in a small lounge half-filled with people. She paused for a moment and then saw Holly, seated in an armchair near a plant-filled window.

"Hi," she whispered, crossing to a nearby chair. "How are you?"

Holly smiled. "Hi. Fine, thanks. I heard you guys partying last night," she said, pulling her skirt down over her knees.

Slightly chagrined, Maddie gave her new friend an apologetic smile. "Sorry—you could hear us?"

Holly rolled her eyes. "I sure could! I live next door to Rogers—in Beekman. But don't worry about it. We'll get our revenge one of these days."

"Remind me to leave town before that hap-

pens," Maddie said, chuckling. She looked up and
noticed a slightly overweight but impeccably
dressed brunette coming toward them, and Holly
waved a greeting.

"Hi, Katie. Katie Winston, this is Maddie Lerner."

Pulling up a chair, Katie nodded and raised a
carefully manicured hand to toy nervously with her
hair. "Hi. Thinking about joining us?"

"Yes. I think it sounds like a lot of fun. And a
great way to be part of Hawthorne."

"Well, it is," Katie agreed as she settled into her
chair. "If you have the time, that is. I swear, all my
professors this semester have assigned twenty-five-
page papers. I think it must be some kind of con-
spiracy. Or else they just enjoy torturing us and
watching us suffer."

Holly snickered and winked at Maddie. "Actually, Katie, my anthropology class is doing a
study on college professors and how they're spir-
itually related to some sadists of primitive cultures.
It's the truth, I swear," she added solemnly, holding up one hand as Katie sent her a pained look.

"Well, on top of that, I'm captain of the debating
team this semester, too, you know," Katie huffed.
"So I'm pretty busy."

"Hi, everyone!" said a petite redheaded girl, ar-
riving with a flourish and shutting the door behind
her. "Sorry I'm late."

Holly leaned close to whisper in Maddie's ear.
"Barbara Hess—she's the president of Gold Key."

Barbara began handing around a stack of papers, and she got the meeting going right away.

Another busy, involved person, thought Maddie. Just like she was going to be.

"Okay, the next couple of weeks are going to be wild," announced Barbara. "Everyone who got accepted this spring will be coming to look around, even if they had a preapplication tour. So we're going to have plenty of business. Plus, the admissions office is organizing activities for a couple of busloads of students coming from high schools around Georgia and South Carolina. Hi, you're a new face," she said suddenly, stopping in front of Maddie.

With a shy smile, Maddie nodded. "Yes. Is it okay if I join late?"

"Are you kidding me?" Barbara let out a snort of incredulous laughter. "Didn't you hear what I just said? We need at least a million new people, so you're more than welcome. What's your name?"

"Maddie."

"Okay, Maddie. Talk to me after the meeting, okay?"

"Sure."

Turning away abruptly, Barbara chirped on. "Okay, this is the revised schedule of events for the rest of the semester, including the admissions office schedule of tours—that doesn't include the individual tours, though." Barbara bounced back into her seat and crossed her legs under her.

"And also—admissions people want us to stress the athletic facilities more. They say people are coming back after their tours with questions about the sports complex, like they didn't get enough info from you guys," she continued with a stern glance around the room. "If you haven't been there enough to be really familiar with it, get hopping. There's a new weight room donated by some illustrious alum that everyone is very proud of, so be sure to point that out."

With growing excitement, Maddie listened to Barbara's fiery enthusiasm and sneaked quick glances down at the schedule in her lap. If she had been looking for ways to find out about campus activities, it was obvious she'd come to the right place. One of her favorite movies, *Terms of Endearment*, was being shown for a psychology class on suffering, and anyone could go. And she was surprised to see there was actually a campus grievance committee that held meetings every Thursday evening. She held back a chuckle when she saw that at the same time there was a meeting of the Optimists' Club.

"Any announcements?" Barbara said, looking around quickly.

A long-legged boy wearing a blue blazer nodded. "Yes—the Hawthorne Republican Club is sponsoring a series of political speakers in May," he drawled, staring intently at his fingernails. "As well as a forum on the state legislature."

"Great, Troy. Anything else?"

"Uh, Barb—this is wrong here on the schedule," said another boy. He pushed his glasses up his nose with a impatient gesture. "The Film Society's double feature next weekend is Bergman's *Seventh Seal* and *Cries of Whispers*, not *Autumn Sonata* like it says. We couldn't get that one from the distributor."

Barbara nodded and made a note on her schedule. "Okay everyone, is that it?"

Scrabbling in her purse for a pencil, Maddie felt herself grinning. Everyone there seemed to be involved in some kind of campus organization in addition to the Gold Key, and she found herself eyeing them with respect. Working with them would be wonderful: she'd find out about everything that was going on at Hawthorne and make some interesting friends in the bargain.

"Okay," Barbara said, pushing back her chair. "As usual, check in with the admissions office whenever you'll be able to take a tour—or if you think you have to cancel. And be sure to give any new phone number in case they need to reach you. Thanks for coming, everyone."

Immediately, Barbara was surrounded by people asking her questions, and Maddie looked at Holly with a wide smile. "She's really something," she said quietly.

"Our fearless leader, you mean?" Holly nodded and rolled her eyes. Maddie smiled and glanced back at her schedule.

"Hey, look!" Katie broke in excitedly. "Roy Anderson, that unbelievably handsome anchorman from channel seven, is speaking to the broadcasting class. Anyone want to go? Holly? Maddie?"

"Sure. I'd love to. He's a very good journalist," Maddie said with sincerity.

Katie pushed herself to her feet and laid a hand on Maddie's arm. "Who cares what he does? It's what he looks like that counts. I'll call you, okay? And we can go together."

"Okay, bye." Turning back to Holly, Maddie said, "I can't wait to do my first tour. It sounds like so much fun."

"Maddie?" Barbara Hess threw herself into the chair Katie had just vacated. "Now, tell me about yourself."

"This is my cue to leave," Holly said with a smile. "See you later, Maddie. Bye, Barb."

"And then she asked if I thought I'd be ready by Monday for my first tour," Maddie explained breathlessly as she reached for a plate of tuna salad and pushed her tray down the line.

Sam grabbed a dish of green beans and stared at the dessert selection. "I think I'll pass," she muttered at the green Jell-O. Then she flashed Maddie a wide smile. "That's great, Mad. I bet you'll be really good at it."

Heading for their usual table, Maddie didn't have much of a chance to say anything else; it took all her energy to keep her tray from being knocked out of her hands in the crowd. Up ahead, she made out Roni's distinctive auburn hair and, one seat over, Stacy's straight gold locks. With a sigh of relief, she maneuvered her way into a chair and sat down.

"Hi, you guys."

Sam set down her tray and slid into a chair next to Stacy. "Listen, if you two ever need a lesson in getting things done, you should see Maddie."

Lifting her eyebrows curiously, Stacy looked across the table at Maddie. "I shouldn't ask what that means," she said wryly. "It might be a thinly veiled hint about my overdue ceramics project."

"You're just paranoid," Roni scoffed, digging into her Reuben sandwich with typical gusto. She stuffed a forkful of corned beef and rye bread into her mouth. After she finished her tremendous bite, she looked at Maddie, feigning concern. "So what's the deal here? Are you, well, are you an over-achiever? Oh, Maddie, say it isn't so!"

Maddie grinned self-consciously and shrugged. "I don't know *what* she's talking about," she said, turning innocent eyes to Sam.

"Yeah, right." As she opened a carton of milk, Sam explained, "Maddie wants to get into campus activities, right? So what does she do? Jumps right into the heart of it—she's giving her first campus tour on Monday."

"No kidding? That's great," Stacy said with a smile. "Did you see Holly at the Gold Key meeting?"

Maddie nodded. "Yeah, and that president, Barbara Hess—she's like a general or something." She chuckled, imagining Barbara in a uniform—it seemed to fit.

Maddie pulled out the schedule Barbara had given her and examined it again as she ate her lunch, her friends chattering around her. Then her eyes fell on one entry, and she paused with her glass of soda halfway to her mouth. "Look at this!" she cried excitedly, putting her glass down on her tray with a bang.

The others looked up expectantly. "Yeeeees?" Roni drawled.

"Today's the first day of tryouts for *A Midsum-*

mer Night's Dream. I didn't even notice this before.
I can't believe it!"

Stacy leaned her elbows on the table and swept
her hair back over one shoulder. "Something tells
me this is a significant event."

"It is. I really want to try out for the play," Maddie explained, opening her pocket datebook and
frowning. After class that afternoon she was meeting Barbara for a practice trip around campus. But
that wouldn't take more than an hour. "Good," she
murmured as she checked her schedule. "I can
make it."

Across the table, her three suitemates exchanged a meaningful glance. Sam cleared her
throat. "Uh, Maddie, I know you want to do this
play, but doesn't it seem like you've got an awful
lot to do?"

Surprised, Maddie met Sam's earnest gaze. Compared to everything there was to do at Hawthorne,
she was barely scratching the surface. "Don't worry
about it, Sam. I can handle it. Besides," she added,
putting her hand on Sam's arm, "I have to make
up for lost time, remember?"

"Well, this girl just puts me to shame," Roni said,
her eyes twinkling. "Maybe I ought to go try out
for the women's diving team or something."

Stacy choked on her water. "Give me a break,"
she gasped, waving her hand in front of her face
as she caught her breath. "The day you try out for
any team, I'm quitting school."

Sam let out a little hoot of laughter, which she
quickly turned into a cough when Roni glared at her.

With a fond chuckle, Maddie looked at her

friends. It was great to feel like part of a group, They all felt so comfortable together. "Hey, I'd better get going, or I'll be late for calculus," she said, suddenly realizing the time. "I'll tell you all about it when I get back from the theater, okay?"

Sam met her eyes again briefly with a slightly worried frown. "Okay. Have fun."

Maddie gathered her books together, and gave Sam a wink as she stood up. "Don't worry, I will."

Come, now a roundel and a fairy song;
Then, for the third part of a minute, hence;
Some to kill cankers in the musk-rose buds,
Some to war with rere-mice for their leathern
    wings,
To make my small elves coats, and some keep
    back
The clamorous owl, that nightly hoots, and
    wonders
At our quaint spirits. Sing me now asleep;
Then to your offices, and let me rest.

"Thank you very much," called out the director from somewhere in the darkened auditorium. The girl trying out for the part of Titania, queen of the fairies, smiled regally and walked off the stage. "Okay! Next Titania, please."

Maddie slumped down farther in her seat, wrinkling her nose. Now that she was there, listening to the students auditioning, she didn't think she could do nearly as well. She was sure she wasn't going to try for any of the leads, at any rate. And she wasn't even sure about the bit parts.

Another girl flitted across the stage and assumed what she apparently thought was fairy queen posture. "Be kind and courteous to this gentleman," she began in a lilting tone. Bored, Maddie craned her neck to look around in the dimly lit theater.

"Kind of violent, don't you think?" came a familiar voice from behind her.

Turning quickly around in her seat, Maddie found herself grinning like a fool as she met Stu Peterson's eyes. "What do you mean?" she asked, puzzled.

He nodded toward the stage. "Didn't you hear that part about cropping the 'waxen thighs' of the 'humble-bees,' and plucking the wings off butterflies?" He shuddered dramatically. "Gives me the creeps," he said with an impish grin.

"I guess you'll say anything when you've been slipped a love potion," Maddie retorted, trying to keep her delighted surprise from showing. Finding Stu Peterson at the same auditions was an unexpected stroke of luck.

Nodding, Stu added, "I guess that's a pretty good excuse. So, what are you trying out for?" He leaned forward to rest his arms across the back of the seat next to Maddie. "No—let me guess. You want to be one of the fairies—Cobweb or Pease-Blossom, right? You've got that sort of look."

"Hmm. I'm not sure if that's a compliment or what," Maddie said. Stu's green eyes were dark and mysterious in the unlit auditorium, and she found herself staring into their depths more candidly than she would in full daylight. She was thrilled when he clambered noisily over the seats to sit next to her.

"Okay," the director called out. "Fairies—anyone for fairies! We need a Mustard-Seed, Moth, Cobweb, Pease-Blossom, plus attendant elves, sprites, pixies, etcetera! All fairies on stage, please. We'll get to Oberon in a minute."

"Here's your chance," Stu whispered.

Maddie giggled. "No, thanks. I'm not really sure if I'm cut out for this." She turned to look at him curiously. "What are you trying out for?"

"I'm not," he said, pulling up his long legs and resting his knees against the back of the seat in front of him. "I want to be stage manager. I'm really more interested in the production end of things than in the acting."

"Oh." Maddie thought fast and nodded. "You know what?"

"What?"

"So am I."

In the light streaming forward from the stage, Maddie could see Stu grinning. "Well, now, isn't that a coincidence?" he said quietly. "Maybe we could have dinner together and discuss your career."

Maddie felt her heart thump. It was exciting, sitting in the dark and flirting with Stu. She knew neither one of them would act like this under other circumstances—from their earlier conversation, she knew that Stu was not the type of boy to come on really strong, and she certainly wasn't that type of girl. Maybe it was being in the theater that was making them act.

"Maddie?"

She jumped and felt herself blushing. "Oh! I'd love to," she whispered.

His hand brushed against her arm as he stood up. "They won't really be doing any production stuff today, anyway—I just came to watch out of curiosity. Do you want to go to the snack bar?"

"Sure," she said, reaching behind her for her sweater and her books. "Let's go."

"There's a lot of running around for props and things," Stu explained as they sat in a booth in the student snack bar. He toyed with his soda, making wet circles on the table top, and threw his blond bangs back out of his eyes in a gesture that Maddie was beginning to know well. "Of course, it's the designer who makes the creative decisions, but a lot of times you have to make up your own mind about what will work and what won't, depending on whether what the designer wants is impossible. And then while the show is running, you have to make sure everything goes smoothly."

Maddie sighed and pushed away her plate. "It sounds like a lot of work, but it sounds like fun, too."

Looking up swiftly, he caught her eye. "You're just saying that. It sounds dumb, and we both know it."

"No, it doesn't!" she protested, shaking her head with a smile. "I really think it sounds like something I'd enjoy—and not for some ulterior motive," she added, blushing and looking down. "I mean it," she repeated. "I'd like to get involved in something like this. I mean, my grades always come first, but I don't have to study all the time."

There was a short silence, and finally Maddie

looked up. Stu was smiling at her, and she found herself smiling back.

"Hey, how about if I walk you home?" he said. "I'm afraid I have a ton of studying to do tonight, so I've got to get going. Otherwise I wouldn't mind staying here for another four or five hours."

She laughed and stood up. "Me too."

All the way back to Rogers House, they talked in a friendly, comfortable way. It was as though they had known each other all their lives, Maddie thought as they reached the front door. Suddenly they were stricken by an awkward silence.

"Well, here we are," she said, feeling stupid as she said it.

He nodded with a lopsided grin. "Yeah. Here we are."

"Thanks for dinner."

"Sure. See you in class, right?"

For a moment Maddie was sure he was going to kiss her, and she caught her breath in anticipation as she looked up into his eyes.

"Hi, Maddie!" Roni called, running up the steps toward them. She noticed Stu and paused. "Hi," she said, darting a questioning glance at Maddie.

"Roni, this is Stu Peterson. Stu, this is Roni Davies, my roommate," Maddie said quickly.

Stu nodded. "Nice to meet you, Roni. See you later, Maddie. Thanks." With a last warm smile, he turned and jogged down the steps.

"Well, well, well," Roni murmured, turning her key in the lock. "We're going to have to hear *all* about this, Miss Lerner."

Chapter 6

"We have returned!" Roni announced as she flung open the door of suite 2C.

On the couch, Stacy and Sam studiously ignored Roni's dramatics. "Do you feel a draft?" Sam asked Stacy with a puzzled frown.

"You know, I think the door must be open. Why, look!" she cried, feigning astonishment as she turned around and saw Roni and Maddie standing in the doorway.

"Hardy har har." Roni stalked into the living room and threw herself into a chair, propping her legs up on the cluttered table. "You guys really know how to make someone feel welcome."

As Maddie dropped her books on the round table, Sam looked over the back of the couch at her.

"I picked up your mail for you, Maddie. There's an airmail letter that your aunt forwarded."

"Oh, thanks." Maddie stepped out of her shoes and picked up the blue envelope, curious. "Hey, it's from my cousin Ellen from South Carolina."

"Since when do you need an airmail stamp to send a letter from South Carolina to Georgia?" Stacy drawled, highlighting a passage in her chemistry book with a bright orange marker.

Tearing open the letter, Maddie quickly scanned the contents, a tender, reminiscent smile on her face. "My cousin got married on Valentine's Day to a guy in the air force named Mark, and they just got transferred to Okinawa," she explained as she squeezed onto the end of the couch next to Sam. "So—airmail."

"Valentine's Day? For real?" Stacy threw up her hands and sent a beseeching look heavenward. "Lord, have you ever heard anything more utterly romantic than that?"

"*Speaking* of which," Roni cut in quickly, meeting Maddie's sudden look of bashfulness with a fiendish grin. "Sorry, Maddie, I can't keep this a secret."

The others perked up. "What?" Sam demanded, flashing an expectant grin at Maddie. "What is it?"

Maddie felt her face redden. "It's nothing—Roni is making a big deal out of nothing."

"She's so modest! I just found her on the steps in a clinch with a very—repeat *very*—cute guy."

"Roni, come on! It wasn't a 'clinch'!"

"Are you serious?" Stacy's mouth dropped open,

and she drew her eyebrows together as she looked at Maddie. "Not Stu Peterson, by any chance?"

Roni crossed her legs with a nonchalant air. "I believe that was the name mentioned."

Sam let out a low whistle. "Now everyone's met this mystery date but me. Madison Lerner, I swear you are the fastest girl I ever met."

"I am not—we just met, and we—" Confused, Maddie looked at each of her suitemates in turn, not knowing how to explain. "We just—"

"No need to explain," Sam said loftily. Then she dissolved into giggles and leaned over to hug Maddie. "We're just teasing you, silly. Don't look so mortified!"

With a sigh of relief, Maddie sank down farther into the couch. "Well, he's pretty nice," she said softly, and meeting Sam's eyes again, echoed her friend's giggles.

"Anybody mind if I put on some music?" Roni asked, leaning over toward the stereo.

Stacy looked up briefly. "Put on something classical, okay? Like Mozart. I'm trying to study."

"You and your Mozart," Roni grumbled, but she selected the tape anyway and popped it into the cassette deck. The soothing, poignant strains of a violin concerto lilted out of the speakers, and Stacy gave a contented sigh.

Stifling a yawn, Maddie reached into her bookbag for her campus map. It was still fairly early, and she could use the time now to study for her first tour. As she spread the map out on her knees, another yawn pried her mouth open, and she raised a hand to her lips.

Sam shot her a look from the corner of her eye. "Not sleepy, are you, by any chance?"

Maddie chuckled wearily and frowned at her map. She could barely keep her eyes open, but she peered intently at it anyway. "At least we don't have Shakespeare on Wednesdays—I can sleep late tomorrow."

"You know what we need to do?" Roni said suddenly, piling her hair on top of her head and looking at the group with an eager smile.

"Find a cure for cancer? Bring about world peace? Make a million dollars?" Stacy shook her head. "I give up."

Roni leaned back over her chair, arching her neck and staring at the ceiling. "Does the phrase 'shopping in Atlanta on Thursday night' mean anything to you?"

Stacy's highlighter stopped moving abruptly, and she raised her eyes to look at Roni admiringly. "Miss Davies, I declare that's the best idea you've had in days."

"Maddie?"

"What?" Maddie looked up from her map and tried to concentrate on Roni and Stacy. "I'm sorry, I wasn't listening."

"That's right—you were sleeping," Sam retorted with a giggle.

Maddie poked her in the ribs. "I was not!" But she snuggled down and put her head on Sam's shoulder. "You don't mind if I just rest my eyes, do you?" she asked, smiling drowsily.

"I said, do you want to go to Atlanta on Thursday night?" Roni repeated.

"The department stores are open late," Stacy explained, fitting the cap on her highlighter with a snap.

Maddie gave them a tired nod. "Sure, that sounds like fun. What time would we leave—after dinner?"

Roni and Stacy exchanged a quick glance.

"Actually," Sam said, not looking up from her book, "when we go, we usually leave after lunch so we can get there in the afternoon. After we shop for a while we have dinner, and then we hit some more stores."

"But—" Maddie wrinkled her brow. She knew she was missing something. "Doesn't that mean skipping afternoon classes?"

Sam nodded. "Yeah." She glanced at Maddie, and a look of surprise crossed her face. "Don't tell me you never cut a class before!"

Shaking her head slowly, Maddie said, "No, I never have."

"Well, for heaven's sake, Maddie!" Roni crowed, leaping to her feet. "You have simply got to learn what your priorities are! I mean, look at me!"

Maddie looked dutifully at Roni, at her midcalf, skintight jeans, her oversized white shirt, and the spangled pink scarf wrapped around her neck. 'Okay, I'm looking."

Roni sent a sardonic grin at Stacy and Sam. "Funny, isn't she?" Still grinning, she swooped down on Maddie and grabbed her shoulders. "Listen. Shopping is one of those things you *have* to do every once in a while—to keep your perspective on school. And besides, you're so far ahead in all your classes, what could it hurt? Relax, lighten up, live a little!" she commanded, her eyes wide with enthusiasm.

"Well . . ."

"That means yes," Stacy said triumphantly. "We'll rendezvous here after lunch."

Maddie smiled as she warmed to the idea. It *did* sound like fun. "Should we synchronize our watches?"

"That *definitely* means yes." Roni laughed and threw herself back into her chair. "Then it's all settled. Maddie Lerner cuts class for the first time on Thursday, and the terrible two C's descend upon Atlanta."

A low chuckle escaped from Sam. "Compared with us, Sherman's march through Georgia will seem like a garden party."

"Don't wear those shoes," Roni warned Maddie as she stepped into a pair of pumps. "We'll be covering a lot of territory."

"Huh?" Maddie looked at her feet, and her mouth twisted in a wry smile. "Hmm, maybe you're right. You don't happen to have a spare pair of army boots, do you?"

Roni punched Maddie lightly on the shoulder. "You're a real comedienne, Lerner. Come on."

They joined Stacy in the living room, and Maddie looked around in surprise. "Where's Sam?"

"Here I am." Sam stood in the door of her bedroom, a wan smile on her face. She was dressed in an old pair of sweatpants and a Mickey Mouse T-shirt.

"You are *not* going to Atlanta like that, are you?" Roni demanded incredulously.

"Hardly! No," Sam shook her head and shrugged. "I realized I have too much work to do, you guys. I'm sort of worried about my Shakespeare paper, so I'm going to work on it while you're all out."

Maddie felt a sinking sensation of disappointment and sat down on the edge of the couch to collect her thoughts. Even though Roni and Stacy were fast becoming her close friends, she still felt a special connection with Sam. It wouldn't be the same without her along.

"Sam, I can't believe you!" Stacy moaned, shrugging into a beautifully tailored raw silk blazer. "Well, I'm warning you, if I see something that would be perfect for you, I'm not getting it."

Sam chuckled and pulled her hair back into a ponytail with an elastic band. "That's okay. You two have overloaded me on shopping this year anyway. But have fun."

"We will, don't worry," Roni said. She stuck her tongue out at Sam and turned to the others. "Okay troops. Forward, march!"

With a laugh, Maddie pushed herself off the couch and sent one last look over her shoulder at Sam. "Are you sure you can't come?" she asked hopefully.

Sam shook her head. "But you go ahead—I know you're far enough ahead on your Shakespeare paper to take a day off. Not all of us can be as organized as you, that's all."

For a moment, Maddie was tempted to tell Sam

the truth—that the work she had done so far on her Shakespeare paper consisted of one page of vague topic ideas. But Roni tugged on her arm, and she smiled ruefully. "Well, we'll be wishing you were there," she called as Roni pulled her to the door. "Bye!"

When they climbed into Stacy's plush Mercedes, chattering excitedly, the Shakespeare paper was pushed to the outer reaches of Maddie's mind. And as Roni slipped a Madonna tape into the dashboard stereo, Maddie forgot entirely about work. They spent the one-hour drive talking and singing, and soon they were winding their way through the outskirts of Atlanta.

"The parking garage on Peachtree will probably be full, but let's try it anyway," Roni suggested as Stacy maneuvered through a busy intersection. Stacy nodded, and Maddie peered through the windows to get her first real glimpse of the famous Confederate city. She had seen the airport, but that was about it. Aunt Fidelia had promised to take Maddie for a tour, but somehow they had never gotten around to it.

"Isn't Peachtree the street Scarlet O'Hara lived on in Atlanta?" Maddie asked, recognizing the name.

Roni grinned over her shoulder from the front seat. "Sure is—but it looks a little different now."

"I'd say so!" Maddie laughed, craning her neck to look up at gleaming skyscrapers. Soon they were pulling into a dimly lit parking garage, where they miraculously found a free space. Scrambling out of the backseat, Maddie adjusted her bag on her shoulder and felt herself smiling with excitement.

Roni and Stacy looked at one another seriously for a moment. "Neiman-Marcus?" Roni asked solemnly.

With a grave nod, Stacy agreed. "Neiman-Marcus."

"Maddie, try this on!" Roni commanded. She was holding out a black angora sweater with a square neck, and Maddie took it eagerly.

"This is nice," she murmured, stroking the cuddly wool with one hand.

"And it would look incredible on you," Stacy said, joining them with an armful of clothes to try on. "You're lucky you can wear black—it's so sophisticated."

"Yeah, that's me!" Maddie chuckled, thinking about the relatively sheltered life she led—glamorous parties were not an everyday occurrence for her like they were for Stacy and Roni. But it was a beautiful sweater, and not *too* expensive. So far, she had managed to resist most of the "bargains" her friends had tried to foist on her at Neiman-Marcus and Macy's. It was possible to have fun shopping without actually buying anything, but after all, she didn't have to deny herself *everything*.

"Okay, sure," she said, following her friends to the dressing rooms. A severe-looking woman counted their items with a suspicious glare, and holding back their giggles, they piled into one dressing cubicle together.

"What a hatchet face," Roni sneered, throwing her load of clothes onto the chair. Quickly pulling her shirt off over her head, she added, "Anybody else getting hungry?"

"Oh, God!" Stacy groaned.

Maddie and Roni whirled around. Stacy was standing in front of the mirror, fumbling with the shoulder pads on the oversized dress she was trying on.

"What's wrong, Stace?" Maddie asked anxiously. "You sound like you're coming down with appendicitis."

"Appendicitis would be better than this!" Stacy growled, frowning sourly at her own reflection. "I swear—this looked great on the hanger, but on me it might as well be a potato sack."

Astonished, Maddie looked at her friend's image in the mirror. Stacy's perfect size-six figure was set off beautifully by the smooth knit dress, and the big shoulder pads gave her a classic 1940s Joan Crawford silhouette.

Roni raised her eyebrows sardonically. "Yeah, it's the most disgusting thing I ever saw, Swanson. Take that thing off before I throw up."

Shooting Roni a stern glance in the mirror, Stacy shrugged and turned her eyes to Maddie. "So, what do you think?"

With a short laugh, Maddie pulled the black angora sweater on over her head. "You don't want *my* advice about clothes, Stacy. But I think it looks great on you." She eyed her own reflection briefly and decided the sweater looked perfect against her delicate pale skin and black hair.

"She's just fishing for compliments," Roni whispered loudly, her green eyes dancing. "Don't play up to her—her ego is huge enough already."

The laughing eyes of all three girls met in the mirror, and they burst into giggles. Then Roni started hiccuping, which made them giggle even more.

There was a loud knock on the locked door of their cubicle. "Everything all right in there, girls?" came the stern voice of the dressing room attendant.

Maddie clamped a hand over her mouth and tried to control her giggles. "Y-yes, fine," she gasped. "Thank you."

The girls looked at each other expectantly, waiting for the woman to go away. After what seemed like an hour, she said, "Well, then. Call me if you need anything." Finally they heard her footsteps recede.

"She probably thinks we're trying to sneak all these things out under our own clothes," Stacy said, her voice dripping with scorn.

"With those shoulder pads, you wouldn't get very far," joked Maddie.

"Come on, let's go eat something, I'm literally starving to death," Roni said as she struggled out of a beaded tunic.

"Me too," Maddie agreed, stripping off the sweater. She looked indecisively at the black sweater, pursing her lips and wondering if forty dollars was really a bargain, or if she was just trying to talk herself into it.

Stacy put a hand on her arm. "Buy it," she said warmly. "It really looked good on you."

With a quick smile, Maddie looked up and met Stacy's eyes. "I guess I will." She laughed and buttoned up her blouse. "Now let's eat, huh?"

Roni opened the door and paused, looking back at them with a devilish glint in her eyes. "Watch this," she said with a wink. Sailing down the corridor, she approached the attendant and gave her a huge, fake smile. "Thank you *so* much for your assistance," she crooned, thrusting the pile of clothes into the woman's arms. "But really, none of these things are really *quite* what I had in mind." With that she strode haughtily out of the dressing room area, leaving the woman openmouthed with surprise.

Following quickly behind her, Maddie and Stacy hung up the things they didn't want and hurried up to the cash register to pay for their clothes. When they caught up with Roni, she was leaning carelessly against a pillar, chatting casually with a store mannequin. "Relax, don't be so stiff all the time," she advised, looking around her with a nonchalant air. "So, meet a lot of guys here?"

Maddie tipped her head to one side and regarded Roni and the mannequin. "What's the dummy's name?"

"Roni Davies," Stacy scoffed, taking Roni by the arm. "Maddie, you get her other side."

Laughing, Maddie looped her shopping bag over the crook of her elbow and took Roni's other arm. The three girls trooped down the aisle toward the escalator, their bags banging against their knees.

"The sooner we get out of here, the better," Stacy whispered to Maddie behind Roni's back. "When she gets hungry, she gets really *weird.*"

"Weirder than usual? Then we'd better get out of here, fast!"

Stacy rolled her eyes as Roni made a passing swipe at a rack of silk scarves. "Down, girl, down!"

"You guys are really bananas, you know that?" Maddie chuckled, as they pushed through a revolving door.

"It's true. Totally true," Roni declared, smiling at Maddie. "And you, Maddie Lerner, are officially one of the bunch. Your life will never be the same again!"

"That's what I was afraid of," said Maddie. "Now, where do we eat? I could go for some deep-dish pizza."

"No, let's skip the main course and go right for dessert," Stacy declared. "There's a great old-fashioned ice-cream place around here somewhere. . . ."

Chapter 7

"Oh, Sam, you should have come!" Maddie cried out as she plopped down on the couch in 2C at ten-thirty. Kicking her shoes off, she added, "There was a sale at Laura Ashley, too. I wish you could have gone with us," she repeated softly.

Sam gave her a rueful smile, then yawned and put down her pen. "Well, at least I got a lot of work done." She looked up as Roni and Stacy staggered in through the door with their boxes and bags. "I guess *you* got a lot of work done, too."

"Don't even speak to me, Samantha Hill," Stacy ordered half-seriously. She dumped her packages on the floor and directed a stern look at her roommate. "Just because you stayed here to be virtuous doesn't give you the right to make me feel guilty."

"What!" Laughing incredulously, Sam shook her head and looked at Maddie. "What did I say?"

"Don't pay any attention to her. She has shopping burnout, something like a really bad hangover."

Sam clicked her tongue with fake sympathy and pouted at Stacy's back. "Poor baby. Oh, I almost forgot," she said, turning back to Maddie with a gasp. "Your parents called a while ago—I wasn't sure if you'd want them to know you were in Atlanta, so I told them you were at the library studying."

"Great. Just what I need right now—to talk to my parents. They seriously expect me to be studying one hundred percent of the time I'm not in class." She closed her eyes wearily but opened them again and said earnestly to Sam, "Listen, thanks for covering for me. I really appreciate it."

"Oh, forget it," Sam mumbled with a modest shrug. She swept back her wheat-colored hair and added, "You would have done the same for me."

Resting her head against the back of the couch, Maddie let out another pathetic groan. "Oh, God. I *really* do not want to talk to them tonight! I'm way too tired to deal with them right now."

"Just get it over with," Roni suggested, pulling a shoebox out of the Neiman-Marcus bag and opening it. She wiggled her little feet into her new shoes and muttered. "If these turn out to be the wrong color for my green dress, I'll shoot myself. Look, Mad, if you don't call back, they'll think the worst—that you're with a *boy.* In his *room."*

"God forbid!" Maddie laughed. With a sigh of

resignation, she made herself get up. She picked up the telephone and dragged it into her bedroom. "Might as well get it over with," she muttered, dialing her home phone number.

She tapped her foot nervously as the distant ringing sounded in her ear. It was cut off abruptly. "Hello?"

"Hi, Mom."

"Maddie? Is that you?"

"Mom, of course it's me."

Maddie heard the click of an extension being lifted and then her father's voice. "Well, young lady, where have you been all evening?"

"Studying," she lied, coiling the phone cord around one finger.

"How's everything going, dear?" her mother continued. "Are you all moved in and everything? Are you sure it won't be too distracting for you?"

"Have you been keeping up with your work?" Mr. Lerner cut in.

"Of course, Daddy," Maddie assured him, her voice slightly strained. She hoped they wouldn't notice how tired she was.

"Good. I'm glad to hear it. And Shakespeare? How's the paper coming along?"

Maddie's eyes stared at a book lying facedown on the floor beside her bed. If there was one time she could wish her parents weren't professors, this was it. Usually, sharing her thoughts about her schoolwork with them was stimulating and fun. But in certain circumstances, it was awkward to have your parents know so much about what you were—or weren't—doing.

"Maddie? Can you hear me?"

She jumped. "Sorry, Daddy. Must be a bad connection. Listen, I can't talk anymore—my roommates are all trying to sleep." Raising her eyes, she saw Sam standing in the doorway, shaking her head with a sympathetic smile. Maddie rolled her eyes. "Go away!" she mouthed pointedly to Sam. Grinning, Sam backed out of the room and shut the door.

"Well, okay, Madison. Call me if you have any questions about your paper, okay?"

"Sure, Dad. Thanks. Bye-bye."

Before he could say anything more, Maddie replaced the receiver in its cradle and flopped over backward on her bed. "Oh, help!"

"Parents," Roni said succinctly, coming into the room with an armload of new clothes. She opened the closet door and began hanging things up. "Did they believe you?" she asked over her shoulder.

Maddie opened her eyes and stared at the ceiling.

"Yeah, I guess so. Ugh. I hate having to lie to them, but I know they'd *never* understand if I told them where we were today."

"Tell me about it!" Roni snorted. "From what you said about them the other night, they'd probably disown you or something."

Giggling, Maddie added, "Or have me committed to a mental hospital." She sighed and rolled over onto her stomach, pulling her pillow under her chin. "But you know, I really should get some work done. I've kind of been goofing off lately."

"Come on! You've only been here for four days.

I think you're entitled to a few seconds to settle in, you know."

"I know." Maddie punched at a lump in her pillow and rested her chin on it again. "But first thing tomorrow, I'm starting that Shakespeare paper. Or at least right after class. Right now, I'm just too tired to do anything."

Roni chuckled and shut the closet door. "Well, after all, you're in training."

"For what, the consumer olympics?"

Her eyes wide, Roni beamed at Maddie. "What a good idea!"

Laughing, Maddie sat up and threw her pillow at Roni. "Oh, go to bed, you moron!"

"Hi. Try the pancakes."

Startled, Maddie looked up into Stu's eyes and tried unsuccessfully to assume a casual air. "Well, if you really recommend them," she said, smiling.

"I do. Definitely." Reaching for a plate on the shelf, he added, "But no bacon—too much cholesterol, bad for your heart."

Maddie grinned and pushed her tray along the rack toward the coffee urns. "No kidding! I'll remember that." As she picked up her breakfast, she knew instinctively that he was going to follow her, and she felt herself smiling as she headed out into the crowded dining hall. As she set her tray down at her usual table, she turned back to him and began introducing her suitemates. He had already recognized Aaron and Zack, who were also there.

"Stu, this is Roni—whom you met the other

night. Stacy you know already, and this is Sam. I
mean, Samantha."

Stu gave them all a friendly smile as he pulled
out a chair for Maddie.

"I'm glad to meet you, Stu," Sam began, stirring
milk into her tea. She shot Maddie a glance from
under her lashes and added, "I've been hearing a
lot about you."

"Oh, yeah?" He raised his eyebrows, looked
from Sam to Maddie, and cocked his head to one
side. "All good, I hope."

Sam hid a smile. "Mostly," she said, trying to
look serious.

Polishing off a glass of orange juice, Stacy
pushed her chair back. "It was nice to see you
again, Stu. I have to go. See y'all later," she called
as she hurried away with her breakfast tray.

"Yeah, me too," Roni said with a grimace. "See
you at lunch." Zack and Aaron stood up at the
same time, saying they had to get to class early.

In a moment, there were only the three of them
at the table, and Maddie felt herself anxiously hoping that Stu and Sam would like each other.

"I hear you do production and stage managing
in the theater," Sam said as she spread a little
packet of grape jelly on a piece of toast. "It sounds
like a lot of work."

"Well, it is, but you don't really notice it—I mean,
it doesn't seem like work when you're doing it."
He turned to Maddie. "What's your schedule today?"

"Oh. Well . . ." She set down her coffee and tried
to think. "I've got Shakespeare first, and then I was

thinking about going to the library to do some work on my paper."

"Mind if I join you?" he asked, taking a bite of his pancakes and deftly catching a drop of syrup in his mouth before it fell off the fork. "I should do some studying myself."

"Uh, sure. I don't mind at all," she stammered, and caught Sam's eye. Her friend was grinning into her tea, and Maddie resisted the temptation to burst out laughing. "I usually study on the fourth floor—in the periodical section."

"Great. I'll see you there."

Maddie heaved a sigh as she realized she had just read the same paragraph for the third time. Impatient, she let her eyes rove around the periodical room, taking in the tall stacks of magazines and racks of newspapers from all over the world. In one corner, students sat huddled in front of microfiche machines, their faces illuminated by a spectral blue glow. Maddie wished she had their assignment, not hers. Shutting her book of literary criticism with a snap, she sat back in her chair and let her chin sink to her chest.

"Hi!" Stu Peterson slid into a chair across the table from her, his face a picture of apologetic regret. "Sorry I took so long, but I had to stop by the theater."

His eyes were dancing as he looked at her, and Maddie thought something unusual must have happened for him to be looking so excited. "What's up?"

"Well . . . let's just say you're talking to the official stage manager for *A Midsummer Night's Dream.*"

"Stu! That's great!" Maddie cried, and then ducked her head as several people swiveled around to stare indignantly at her. "That's great!" she repeated in a whisper, grinning from ear to ear.

"Oh, it's nothing," he replied with an air of exaggerated modesty. "Actually, I *am* pretty excited about it," he admitted, his mouth twisting in a self-mocking smile.

Maddie leaned forward on her elbows, her vivid blue eyes wide with enthusiasm. "I really think it's terrific, I don't care what you say. Is there anything a lowly peon like me can to do help?"

"I might be able to find something you can do," he murmured, meeting her eyes. Suddenly he was serious, and he glanced at the books piled around her. "Hey, I'm sorry," he said, sounding concerned. "You came here to study, and I'm just wasting your time."

"No, it's okay. Really."

"Well . . ." Stu sighed and looked up with a smile. "Even so, I don't want to be a pain."

Pushing her books away with a disdainful grin, Maddie shook her head. "Listen, I've always been supercompulsive about my work. It's good for me to have interruptions. I'm *serious,*" she added as she noted the skeptical expression in his eyes.

He laughed. "Okay, I believe you. But I also have to go to class."

Maddie gulped. "Oh, God—is it time already? I have to go to macro. I really hate thinking about inverse inflation curves and the gross national product when I'm supposed to be studying Shake-speare. They don't exactly mix well."

"Yeah, I know. I took macro first semester, and on the final I had to solve Great Britain's economic problems in three hours. I'm not sure why, but Margaret Thatcher hasn't been calling me for ad-vice lately—go figure." As Maddie laughed, Stu rose to his feet and leaned forward across the table on his hands, meeting her eyes. "How about a movie tonight? The film society is showing *Harold and Maude.*"

"I'd like that," Maddie said softly, feeling the color steal across her cheeks.

He grinned. "Okay—how about if I meet you there at quarter of eight?"

"Sure." Maddie watched Stu as he picked up his books and maneuvered around the tables to the door. As soon as he disappeared, Maddie looked back at her Shakespeare books and made a face. Her paper was still just a jumble of half-formed ideas: she had accomplished next to nothing in the library and obviously she wouldn't be doing any work that night.

But it is Friday night, she reminded herself. Not a night to study, but a night to relax and have fun. She knew she could never have said no to Stu's invitation, even if she had wanted to. Her paper would get done—soon. But not tonight.

When Maddie opened the door of the suite after brunch on Saturday, all three of her suitemates were sitting around the living room. The stereo was tuned to the campus radio station, and a melancholy ball was playing softly.

"Well, if it isn't the social butterfly of Hawthorne College," Roni said, looking up from a magazine with a provocative grin.

"Ha ha." Maddie shrugged out of her light jacket and draped it over the back of a chair. She had met Stu earlier in the morning for a long walk, and then they had sat alone at brunch, just talking.

"What's on your agenda for the day, Maddie?" Sam asked, shifting on the couch to look over the back at Maddie.

"Well . . ." Her Shakespeare paper was calling her name, but Maddie closed her ears to its insistent nagging. The closer the deadline got, the harder it became to face it. "I have a calculus quiz on Monday, so I should be reviewing for that," she said, crossing to the window and leaning against the frame. She looked yearningly out across the lake and then turned away, mustering all her willpower. "I really have to study today."

"Well, we all do," Roni put in with an ironic drawl. "Theoretically, we should be studying all the time—we're in college, don't forget."

Stacy laughed loudly and opened a bottle of nail polish. "How can we?" Carefully stuffing cotton between her bare toes, Stacy began lacquering her toenails with a shade of pearly pink. Her forehead was creased in concentration, and the odor of nail polish permeated the room. Maddie watched her absentmindedly.

"Hey," Roni chirped, sitting up straighter in her chair. "This month's quiz in *Cosmo* is called 'Does

Your Mate Really Understand You?' Who wants to do it? Sam?"

"No, thanks!" With a sarcastic laugh, Sam shook her head. "Aaron and I are doing just fine—but if I take one of those stupid quizzes, I'll probably find out that we should never see each other again."

Roni curled her lip derisively. "Chicken."

"That's me." Sending Roni another angelic smile, Sam turned back to her book.

Maddie caught Roni's eye and put up her hands. "Don't look at me!" She quickly grabbed her calculus book off the table and slid down along the wall, leaning her back against it. Opening the book, she added, "I'm busy studying, see?"

"And it's about time, too, my dear," Roni commented wryly. "I was beginning to think you studied in your sleep or something."

Sam raised her eyes. "You know, I don't know how you do it—you've got the best grade point average of all of us, but you also find time to do so many interesting things."

"And on top of all that, she's got nice teeth," Stacy put in unexpectedly.

The others turned to her in surprise. "What do you mean, nice teeth?" Maddie asked with a puzzled grin. "They're no better than anyone else's."

Stacy shrugged and moved the tiny brush to another nail. "It's just that they look real—you know?"

Self-consciously, Maddie ran her tongue along her front teeth and shook her head. "If you say so," she said, smiling uncertainly. "But they really don't help with calculus."

"Don't pay any attention to her," Sam advised solemnly. "The fumes must be going to her brain. But seriously, I really admire the way you fit everything in. You always seem to have time to do what you want to do, and I've got to work like a maniac to get this stupid paper done." She rolled her eyes. "You're probably already finished, knowing you."

A faint flush swept up Maddie's throat, and she fiddled awkwardly with the corner of one page, bending it back and forth into a limp dog ear. How Sam ever got the impression she had done so much work on her Shakespeare paper was beyond her—but at this point it would be pretty embarrassing to admit she hadn't even gotten beyond the idea stage. She shrugged and muttered, "It's no big deal."

"Well, I'm going to try to be more like you and make time for *me*—do some interesting things instead of holing up in my room with books all day." Nodding decisively, Sam tossed her book onto the floor. "So there. Who wants to go to the Texas Taco for dinner and see a movie tonight? Maddie? Or are you going out with Stu again?"

"No-o. We didn't make any plans." She'd heard of the Texas Taco, even though she'd never been there, and it was supposed to be a lot of fun. She had heard it was decorated with fake cactus and dusty piñatas, and the waiters all wore green-and-yellow sombreros. She had planned to spend the evening in the library, though. She had to make some serious headway on her Shakespeare paper.

"Well, how about it?"

"I really . . . I don't know. What's the movie?"

Sam gave her a delighted grin. "Psi Omega House is showing *Bringing up Baby,* the one where Cary Grant and Katharine Hepburn fall in love while taking care of a leopard."

"Bringing Up Baby!" Maddie groaned, tossing her book aside in a gesture of defeat. "It's one of my all-time favorite old movies."

"Wellllll?"

With a weak smile, Maddie looked up to meet Sam's expectant gaze. "Sure I'll go," she said, swallowing hard. "It'll be fun."

Chapter 8

"Hi—I'm Maddie Lerner. I'm supposed to be taking a group around campus," Maddie said hesitantly as she stepped into the admissions office.

A petite, white-haired secretary nodded at a chair. "Take a seat—the family's still interviewing with Ms. Feinstein, but they'll be out in a minute. They're from *Nashville*," she added in a hoarse whisper.

With a fleeting smile, she turned back to her typewriter and tapped away at a furious pace. Maddie sat down awkwardly on the edge of a chair and crossed her legs. Next to her on a small end table was a selection of brochures. "Welcome to Hawthorne College" and "Adjusting to College Life" were some of the titles. Maddie pulled her skirt down a bit over her knees and looked apprehensively at the door. Now that she was there, waiting for her first tour, she was overcome with nervousness. Not that she didn't know her stuff— in fact, she'd spent most of Sunday reading and studying to prepare for this tour. But still . . .

An enthusiastic voice suddenly became audible as the door to the inner office opened, and Ms. Feinstein, the director of admissions, stepped out, speaking over her shoulder to someone inside. "I'll just see if your Gold Key Guide is here," she called.

Maddie stood up quickly and came forward.

"Are you—Madison Lerner?" Ms. Feinstein asked, leaning over the desk to consult a schedule briefly.

"Yes, I am."

The woman flashed her a friendly smile and nodded. "Cynthia Labriola and her family are ready for their campus tour now," she said briskly, heading for her office again. "I'll just tell them you're here."

Introductions were made, and Maddie led the Labriola family out into the warm April sunshine. "I should confess right at the beginning that this is my first tour," she said with a smile. "So if I'm not showing you or telling you what you were hoping for, just let me know."

Cynthia Labriola, a tiny girl with brown, curly hair, nodded and returned Maddie's smile shyly. "I'm interested in everything, I guess," she said, darting a quick glance at her mother.

"But especially in the music program," Mrs. Labriola said. She put one hand on Cynthia's thin shoulder and squeezed. "Cindy has taken voice lessons for years, and hopes to continue in college. Everyone says she has a remarkable voice. Don't they, sugar?"

A fiery blush swept over the girl's cheeks, and Maddie felt a surge of compassion for her. This seemed to be a clear case of parental ambition, something Maddie was pretty familiar with herself. Out of nowhere came an old memory: her mother bragging about her as Maddie made the finals of a statewide, fourth-grade spelling bee. Parents were the same all over, it seemed. She warmed to the high school girl and felt as if she knew her already. "All right," she said, nodding toward the south end of the campus. "We can start with the Fine Arts Complex, then. That's where music classes, student recitals, and practice rooms are."

She led them down a shady path and continued talking, congratulating herself on the hours of preparation she had invested. On Sunday night she had even asked Sam to quiz her on campus facts. "There are thirty baby grand pianos on campus," she told them proudly. "Some are in a few of the dormitories—for parties and things. But most of them are in the music building. And there's one concert grand in the big auditorium."

"Isn't that wonderful, darlin'?" Mrs. Labriola crooned, casting a triumphant look over her shoulder at her husband. So far he hadn't said a word, and even now he just grunted noncommittally and sneaked a quick glance at his watch.

Maddie suppressed a smile and turned slightly to Cynthia, who was walking at her side. "Well, here we are."

* * *

"Good-bye! I hope you come to Hawthorne next year!" Maddie called, waving farewell as the Labriolas climbed into their station wagon.

The woman's voice, now painfully familiar, drifted out the open window. "Wasn't she charming, Cindy? I told you you'd meet nice girls here, didn't I?" Maddie had a last glimpse of Mrs. Labriola still chattering nonstop over the headrest to her daughter, just as Cynthia turned to smile back at Maddie, lifting her hand in a quick wave.

As the car disappeared down the sweeping drive, Maddie let out a long sigh of contentment. There was no question in her mind that she had done a good job. *A very good job,* she repeated to herself with satisfaction.

Shaking her head with a little smile, Maddie turned and walked slowly down the steps toward Rogers House. The sun slanted through a pair of stately white pines, and she walked under them, feeling the springy needles beneath her feet. It was almost three o'clock, and it was definitely time to get going on that Shakespeare paper, she told herself firmly.

"Hey, Maddie! Wait up!"

Startled, Maddie stopped and looked back. Down the steps of Wagner Reception Center came Holly Dieter, waving frantically.

"Hi, did you just have a tour?" Holly panted as she jogged up. "I saw you leaving Wagner, but I was talking to my sociology professor. So I couldn't exactly yell for you to wait for me."

The two girls fell into step together, and Maddie smiled. "No, I guess you couldn't."

"So, how did it go?"

"Pretty well, I think. At least, they seemed to enjoy it. That's what counts, I guess."

Holly nodded. "Yeah. Hey, I'm on my way to the snack bar to watch *GH*. Do you want to come?"

"*GH?* What's that?"

Holly let out a short laugh. "Don't tell me you aren't a fan of *General Hospital?* It's practically an admission requirement here, you know."

Maddie stared openmouthed at the other girl. "Oh, come on—you can't be serious? You spend your time watching soap operas?"

"Absolutely!" Holly laughed. "Come on, why don't you come with me? There's a whole bunch of us that usually watch together on the TV in the student lounge. We eat french fries and ice cream, drink a lot of diet soda, and try to guess what improbable twists and turns the plot will take. It's a great way to relax every afternoon."

For a moment, Maddie was still not sure if Holly could be serious. Of all the ridiculous things to waste time on, soap operas had to be the worst. She cocked her head to one side and gave Holly a lopsided grin. "Are you totally serious?"

Holly snorted with laughter and took Maddie's arm. "Well, see for yourself what we ambitious, dedicated, serious-minded Hawthorne students do at three o'clock every afternoon."

"Okay! If you insist!" Maddie let herself be led away and shook her head, giggling. "You have got to be crazy, Holly. I can't believe anybody really watches the soaps at school."

But when they arrived in the TV lounge at the snack bar, there were dozens already there, their eyes on the big-screen television. The room was filled with chattering voices, and people moved around busily, jockeying for good seats. Someone pushed past Maddie and Holly where they stood by the door and sat down in the middle of the floor with a heaping plate of french fries slathered with ketchup.

"Come on, there's a free space in the corner." Holly motioned toward a pile of cushions spread on the floor, and they picked their way across the crowded room. Suddenly every voice was hushed, and the first scene of *General Hospital* started.

"Trust me, you'll enjoy this," Holly whispered, lighting a cigarette.

"Okay," Maddie said, chuckling. Determined to be a good sport about it, she turned her full attention to the show. Clearly, most of the kids there took the soap opera with a grain of salt—people spoke out loud to the characters or let out groans of anguish at the really absurd situations and unlikely exchanges. During a commercial, Holly ran out to the snack bar and came back with a plate of fries and two diet sodas.

"I can't wait to see if those tests come back from the lab today," Holly said as the action started up again.

Momentarily confused, Maddie frowned. Did Holly mean she was sick? she wondered. Then it dawned on her. "Oh, you mean—"

"On the show, silly."

"Can you believe this guy?" groaned a girl in the corner. "This is the stupidest plot twist yet."

"No—remember the ice princess stuff a few years ago?" someone else called out. "Totally bizarre."

One of the characters on the screen walked slowly toward a closed door, and everyone in the lounge started calling out warnings to him. "Don't do it!"

"You'll regret it, Steve!"

Holly closed her eyes in despair. "I do not believe this is happening."

Maddie found that she was actually becoming absorbed in the show, in spite of the corny music and terrible overacting. That all made it more enjoyable somehow, and as she licked salt off her fingers, she realized that it was more than just the show itself that made the experience fun. It was the companionship of the people crowded into the room, and the shared sense of interest in the lives of these fictional characters. She leaned back contentedly and stole a quick glance at Holly. Living on campus was full of surprises, but she was having a good time finding out what they were.

A tense silence hung over the room as two of the main characters faced off in the parking lot, their eyes filled with mutual hatred. The music reached a fever pitch of suspense, and then the action froze and the credits began rolling up the screen. Groans of half-serious anger rose up from the group, and people began speculating eagerly about what would happen the next day. All around the room, students began to gather their books together and stand up, and Maddie heaved herself up off the floor.

"So?" Holly asked pointedly as she stood up and straightened her skirt. "Did that hurt very much?"

"Well, it did offend my sense of intellectual integrity," Maddie admitted, trying to look grave. "See you here tomorrow?"

Crowing with laughter, Holly tossed her empty cup into a big garbage can. "Same time, same channel!"

Chapter 9

"That's the last of them," Maddie said as she hung up the phone. She put a check mark next to the name of a local newspaper and smiled across the desk at Stu. "On Saturday we'll have about ten zillion children here to try out for the little fairies. Are you sure we couldn't have just put notices in *one* paper?"

Stu shook his head thoughtfully and flipped over a page of the sheaf of papers he was reading. All around him were scattered empty coffee cups, paperback copies of *A Midsummer Night's Dream*, and pages of scribbled notes. As stage manager, Stu was responsible for overseeing many of the minute details of the production.

"We have the budget to make costumes for twenty-five fairy children of assorted sizes. And I

104

don't know how many we'll have to look at first. Besides," he added, looking up with his familiar quirky grin, "don't you think it'll be kind of fun? All those little kids and their mothers running up and down the aisles and screaming?"

"Fun?" Maddie rolled her eyes and tossed her pencil onto the cluttered desk. "You have some strange ideas about fun, Peterson."

"Well-l-l-l . . ."

Maddie raised her eyebrows inquisitively, her mouth curving into a smile. "Yes?"

Glancing at the clock, Stu said, "Well, would you consider it fun to go get something to eat? The Union closes in about forty-five minutes."

Aghast, Maddie looked at the clock and then at her own watch for confirmation. "Eleven o'clock! You've got to be kidding. I can't believe it's so late—I thought it was still more like nine or something."

"I'm sorry—I didn't mean to keep you so long." Stu slapped his forehead and winced. "And you said you were going to do some work on your Shakespeare paper tonight! I'm really sorry, Maddie. I just got so carried away with what we were doing."

"It's okay—really," she assured him with a smile, touched by his remorse. It made her glad she had spent the whole evening with him. "There's still plenty of time to get it done."

"You sure? When is it due?"

Maddie dropped her eyes and shrugged casually, "A week from Thursday."

"A week from *tomorrow?* Maddie, you better

get going! How much work do you have left to do on it?"

"Almost none," she lied. Seeing that he doubted her a little, she added as convincingly as she could, "Come on! I mean it—I'm almost done. I have never turned in a paper late, and I'm not about to start now. I'll get it done during the day, that's all."

He regarded her uncertainly. "I don't know. . . ."

"Really, Stu," she insisted, reaching across the desk to put a hand on his arm. "I want to help you out on this play, I *really* do. So let's not talk about it anymore, okay?" she added, a trace of stubbornness in her voice.

Still looking doubtful, he shrugged. "Okay, if you say so."

"I do! Now let's go get something to eat before it's too late!"

Stu laughed. "Okay, okay! You win."

Throwing her book bag over her shoulder, she continued, "I'm going to help you as many nights as I can—just not tomorrow night. I'm going to a slide presentation at the library all about manuscript and book preservation, and I'm not sure how long it will last."

As he opened the theater office door, Stu switched off the light. In the darkness Maddie heard him mutter, "How you find the time to sleep, I'll never know."

She chuckled and followed him out into the empty theater. With the schedule she had made for herself, Maddie *was* busy. But she wouldn't have it any other way. She was having too much fun to worry about it.

She gave Stu a playful shove and nodded toward the outside door at the end of the hall. "Come on. Let's get going."

On Friday afternoon, Roni came out of the bathroom dressed in sweatpants and a T-shirt, a pink terry towel wrapped around her head in a turban. She flung herself dramatically onto the couch. "Ahh ..." She let out an agonized sigh and threw her arm across her eyes.

Glancing up from her Greek history book, Maddie met Stacy's eyes. Stacy shook her head slightly, and Maddie ducked her head, grinning. The sound of Sam typing came from the next room, faintly audible over the low music on the stereo.

"Ahhh! ..." Roni groaned again.

Casually, Maddie turned a page in her textbook. Stacy's pencil scratched softly on a sheet of looseleaf paper. Seconds ticked by without a word.

"Hey, come on, you guys, *no fair!*" Roni sat up and directed two indignant glares at her suitemates. "Aren't you even going to ask what's wrong?"

Maddie turned another page and shook her head decisively. "Nope."

"Hey, you guys!" Sam yelled from behind the bedroom door. "Is 'commitment' spelled with two t's and two m's or one of each or what?"

"One m, two t's" Stacy called over her shoulder.

"Two m's, one t," corrected Maddie. She met Stacy's eyes and shrugged.

"Thanks!" Sam called.

On the couch, Roni huffed dejectedly. "You don't care about me, none of you."

"Okay!" Maddie laughed. "What's *wrong,* Roni? *Please* tell me," she said in an anxious tone.

Roni nodded her head politely. "Thank you for asking," she said, her voice all sweetness. "At least *someone* around here seems to care. You want to know what's wrong?" With a characteristically dramatic flourish, she whipped the towel off her head. *"This!"*

For a moment, Maddie and Stacy just stared. Then Maddie clapped one hand to her mouth to keep herself from laughing. Roni's hair was a vibrant, gleaming orange, almost tangerine in color.

Stacy gulped loudly. "Oh, my God, Roni. What did you do?"

"Pretty ghastly, huh?" Roni sighed and propped her legs up on one arm of the couch. "It's a new hair-coloring kit called Razamataz or something stupid like that. I thought I'd give it a try. But I guess my hair had some kind of weird reaction to it."

"Oh, Roni, how could you?" wailed Stacy, who was obviously more upset than Roni was. She came over to the couch and fingered Roni's new tangerine-colored hair with a look of horror on her face. "You've practically ruined your hair!"

"Well, I didn't exactly expect it to turn out this way, you know!" Roni said dryly.

"Give me the phone, Roni."

"What are you doing?" Roni asked, handing her the phone. "Calling the board of beauty on me? Turning me in for hair fraud?"

As she dialed, Stacy said simply. "We've got to fix it right away, that's all. I know a salon in town that can do it now, if I ask. It's where I went to get my hair fixed when I wrecked it last semester. I've gone there a couple of times since then.

Roni shot Maddie a sardonic look. "It's awfully big of her to trust her hair to anyone outside Boston or New York City, don't you think?"

Stacy waved her hand impatiently for silence. "Hello, Etienne? *Bon jour, c'est moi*—Stacy." There was a pause while Stacy listened, smiling and nodding. "*Oui.* My friend Veronica has had a little disaster with her hair, Etienne. We need to come down right away—she needs a one-way ticket back to *auburn. Non*, not Alabama. *Oui. Ah . . . merci beaucoup, Etienne! Au revoir.*"

Hanging up the phone with a flourish, Stacy turned to the others and bowed. "*Voilà!*"

"Oh, great," Roni drawled. "When does the fabulous Etienne come to my rescue?"

"Right now. Hurry up, he has to catch a plane to Aspen tonight."

"Right now?" Roni repeated, leaning back and closing her eyes. "I can't believe this is happening," she muttered. "Okay. Okay, let's go. Maddie, are you coming along for moral support?"

Maddie, who had been watching and listening in amused silence, glanced down at the book in her lap. "Well . . . I don't know."

"Please! You have to come. If I'm there all alone with Stacy and Etienne jabbering away in French, I'll turn into a croissant or something. Please!" she begged in mock desperation as she fell to her knees in front of Maddie and grabbed her legs.

Maddie raised her eyes to Stacy's. "Pitiful, isn't it? A big girl like Roni afraid of the French language. All right." She sighed and shut her book without a second thought. "If you're going to make such a scene, I guess I'd better come."

"Great." Roni jumped up and raced for the bedroom. In a moment she was back, struggling into her sneakers as she hopped on one foot. "Let's go."

"You know," Roni said later through a mouthful of pizza, "that guy A-T-N is not half-bad." She gestured with her slice of super-Sicilian and took another bite with difficulty. "In fact, maybe I'll let him cut my hair the way he wanted to next time. It sounded great. Too bad he had to catch that plane. I was ready to go for it right then and there, you know."

"Well of course he's good," Stacy said, swirling the ice around in her glass. "I keep trying to get Sam to go to him."

Maddie gasped and choked slightly on her soda. "Wh-why?" she stammered when she finally caught her breath. "Sam has absolutely gorgeous hair."

"Of course she does, but I know for a fact she's worn it the same way all her life. She could stand a change."

"No kidding—a change from work, at least," Roni said. "I can't believe she wouldn't come with us—I mean, Friday night and she's still working on this stupid paper? I mean, give me a break."

Daintily picking the anchovies off a slice of pizza

with a knife and putting them on her plate, Stacy nodded. "Really. At least Maddie here knows when to work and when not to." She cocked one eyebrow at Maddie. "But you were probably done weeks ago, and that's why you have so much time to go tearing off to all those things you keep talking about."

"Are you kidding?" scoffed Roni, rolling her eyes. "This girl had all her work done for college before she even graduated from high school. She planned it that way so she'd have time to go out every night and get to every event on the Hawthorne campus."

Smiling slightly, Maddie took a long drink of her soda and stared for a moment into the bottom of the glass. As of this afternoon, she had less than a week to get that Shakespeare paper finished—and she still hadn't even started. And on top of that, she had a paper to research for her classical Greek history class, and a quiz in econ to prepare for—in addition to all her extracurricular plans. She *had* to hit the library over the weekend, maybe even camp out there.

Tomorrow, she told herself firmly. *First thing tomorrow.*

"Who wants that last slice?" she asked.

The silence of the library hung over Maddie like a heavy, smothering cloud. On Saturdays the library was usually deserted, except for the hard-core grinds who never left. Sighing impatiently, she tapped her pencil on the table, trying to concentrate on the passage of criticism she was trying to base her paper on. After a few more fruitless minutes, she put the book down and looked around. Maybe it was too quiet. Maybe if she tried to work at home she'd make more progress. But she knew that wouldn't work—when she was with her suitemates, there were too many other interesting things to be doing. Going back to the dorm was definitely not the answer.

Her mind leaped ahead to the beginning of the week. She had another tour on Monday afternoon. Then to meet Holly to watch GH—no, television was out until the paper was done, she decided firmly. But it *was* such a good way to relax. Besides taking just one hour off a day couldn't possibly make a difference in whether she got the paper done or not. In fact, sometimes it was better to get away from work for a while to recharge your batteries.

Her eyes fell on the desk in front of her, and her smile froze. The scattered books and blank notebook page were a silent reproach, and she turned away in disgust, a hot flush creeping up her throat.

"I'm not getting anything done!" she said aloud, rising to her feet. She pushed a lock of her dark glossy hair behind one ear and pressed her lips together firmly. "There's no point in trying to work when I can't concentrate—it's just counterproductive."

For a moment she stared doubtfully at the table. Then she squared her shoulders and pulled her books together in a pile. Maybe seeing a movie would help. Or better yet, just enjoying the beautiful spring weather that she was missing cooped up in the library. And if she didn't want to get overtired because of everything she was doing she would probably have to take a nap, too. Well, her Shakespeare paper had already waited this long: it could wait another day.

Chapter 10

"I can't believe I did this," Maddie groaned, dropping her head onto her arms. "How could I be so stupid? What am I going to do?"

It was Wednesday night, and Maddie was frantic. Her paper was due in just over twelve hours, and all she had to show for her efforts were five scrawled pages of rambling, inconclusive comments about the use of prophecy in *Macbeth*. Her knuckles whitened as she gripped her pen, and she stared in disbelief at her work.

She lifted her head and looked wildly around the bedroom she shared with Roni. There was no sign of her roommate, who had disappeared on a mysterious errand with Zack shortly after dinner. Stacy, she knew, was in the ceramics studio, working on a new project. For a moment Maddie was so nervous she thought she was going to be sick to her stomach.

Taking a deep breath, she got up from her desk and crossed the room. Maybe Sam could help her. Sam was always so level-headed, so reasonable, so sympathetic. Sam would know what to do.

The living room was empty, and there was no sound from the other bedroom. Her hopes sinking, Maddie opened the door and poked her head in. Sam was gone.

Feeling utterly alone, Maddie walked over to Sam's bed and dropped down onto it, gripping the bedspread with her hands and closing her eyes. She had to stay calm, or she would never get this paper done by morning. As she opened her eyes, she looked bleakly around the room, hoping that Samantha would suddenly materialize and help her out of this crisis. Finally, out of curiosity, her eyes came to rest on Sam's desk.

Maddie clenched her teeth and walked dejectedly over to Sam's typewriter. Next to it, neatly covered in a clear plastic folder, was Sam's paper. After a quick glance into the living room, Maddie picked it up and read through the opening paragraph. Without question, all the long hours Sam had labored over her paper had paid off. The main theme of the paper was well thought out and very interesting. Maddie read on.

Twenty pages later, she lowered Sam's Shakespeare paper and stared blindly into space. There was absolutely no way she could write that good a paper in one night—and that was what Professor Harrison expected. She groped for the chair and pulled it out, lowering herself into it like a feeble old woman.

"What am I going to do?" she repeated aloud. Never in her life had she felt so lost and helpless. Never in her life had she failed to do a superior job on a school assignment. And now, she had failed to do it at all. Period.

Her blank gaze focused on a hastily scribbled note on the desk. It was in Stacy's handwriting. "Sam—Aaron called—he said meet him at eight for the rally, he has to be there earlier than he thought."

The rally. Maddie shook her head stupidly, trying to figure out what that meant. And then it came back to her. Sam's boyfriend had helped to organize a political rally about runaway Defense Department spending, and Sam had been talking about the speakers they had lined up for days. It was scheduled for that night and was expected to last several hours. Sam would be gone until at least ten-thirty.

Almost hypnotized, Maddie watched herself stand up with Sam's paper in her hand and cross to the door. If she stopped to think about it, she couldn't go through with it. But if she didn't do it, she'd fail the class, and that was something she just couldn't afford to do. She hurried to her own room and grabbed her wallet, then slipped out of the suite, heading for the library—and the copying machine on the first floor.

Half an hour later Maddie replaced Sam's paper, carefully aligning it with the typewriter so that Sam wouldn't know if the paper had been moved even a fraction of an inch from where she had put it. Then Maddie lifted her eyes and caught her own reflection in the mirror above Stacy's bureau. Gazing back at her were the eyes of a thief, a cheat, and Maddie turned away quickly.

"Sam would understand," she muttered defensively, feeling the color burn in her cheeks. "She's always helping me out, covering for me, saying that's what friends are for. If she was here, she would say it's okay," she insisted, not feeling very convinced. She headed for the door.

In the middle of the room she stopped and shook her head emphatically. I can't do this, she thought. I can't do this to Sam.

But the thought of admitting to her professor that her paper wasn't done—explaining to her father that her failure to get an A in Shakespeare was because she just never got around to doing her term paper . . . How could she tell her father that of all her classes, she somehow picked *this* one to make a total mess out of?

"I can't," she breathed. Of all the options, explaining to Sam was definitely the least horrible to imagine. But on the other hand, did she even have to do that? After all, they were in different discussion sections for the big class, which meant they would be handing in their papers to different teaching assistants. So no one would ever realize what she had done. There was no reason Sam even had to know! And if Sam ever wanted to read her paper, she could make some excuse and put her off.

The situation seemed much brighter than it had a few moments earlier, and Maddie relaxed her shoulders in relief. Granted, she was doing a really rotten thing, but nobody would be hurt, and nobody would ever have to know. Besides, it wasn't as if she were going to copy it word for word—she was only planning to use it as a guideline.

The words on the photocopied page blurred as Maddie tried to focus her exhausted eyes for the thousandth time. The basement study rooms in Rogers House were hot and stuffy, and the fluorescent lighting was humming monotonously. Maddie shook her head and swayed slightly in her chair. She glanced at her watch: it was just after three-thirty. It seemed like time was barely moving, as if this nightmarish experience would go on forever, and she would still be stuck down in the basement, her fingers stumbling over the typewriter keys.

By now she was copying whole blocks of text from Sam's paper. Her mind was far beyond the point where it could come up with a coherent thought of its own. And she was beyond caring, too. Her paper was sprinkled with dozens of typographical errors, and she couldn't stop to correct them as she made them. The small, caked brush from a bottle of correction fluid lay forgotten on the floor under her chair.

Finally she typed the last page. It didn't even matter that she was done: she couldn't feel very much satisfaction about it. Hands trembling with fatigue, she ripped the photocopy of Sam's paper into tiny shreds and buried them at the bottom of the garbage can. Then she stooped down to unplug her typewriter. The thought of lugging it upstairs filled her with dread.

"You can stay here," she mumbled, straightening up and giving her typewriter a disgusted look from her half-closed eyes. She fumbled the typewritten sheets together and plodded heavily to the door. It was done. That was all that mattered.

"Maddie, Maddie, wake up!"

Slowly she opened her eyes and felt a sickening jolt as she saw Sam's face smiling down at her, all sunshine as usual. Sam was absolutely the last person in the world she wanted to see that morning. She rolled over onto her side and buried her head in her pillow.

"Come on." Sam laughed and jumped onto the bed, jiggling Maddie's shoulder remorselessly. "Time to rise and shine."

"I can't. I—I feel sick."

"What do you mean, sick? Like you're coming down with something, or like you just don't want to get up?"

"Mmmm. Both." Maddie opened her eyes under her pillow. Pale morning light filtered in around the puffy edges. Why did Sam always have to be so nice? Her kindness made Maddie feel a spark of irrational anger. "I don't know," she mumbled halfheartedly.

The bed creaked as Sam stood up. "Well . . . do you want me to take your paper to Shakespeare class?"

˙"No!" In a surge of panic, Maddie sat bolt upright in bed, staring wildly at Sam. She swallowed
hard as her friend looked at her in surprise. "I
mean, I'll make it to class—just go on to breakfast
without me, and I'll see you later."

"Are you sure?" Worry creased Sam's forehead,
and she looked intently into Maddie's face. "I don't
know—maybe you should go to the infirmary or
something, and have one of the nurses check you
over."

"No, I'll be okay," Maddie insisted breathlessly,
averting her eyes from her friend's worried face.
"I'll just take some aspirin—but I don't feel like eating, so go on without me."

Sam still hesitated.

"Go on," Maddie urged desperately. Drawing a
deep breath, she tried to appear normal. "Really,
go ahead," she repeated with a tiny, halfhearted
smile.

"All right, all right." Sam sounded a little aggra-
vated, and she closed Maddie's door a little more
firmly than necessary. Then the door of the suite
banged shut in the living room.

Sighing heavily, Maddie pushed back the covers
and swung her legs out from under the sheet. For
a moment she sat on the edge of her bed, staring
at the floor. Everything that happened the night
before seemed like a terrible dream. She just
couldn't believe she had actually done it. But she
had, and she couldn't undo it an hour before class.
She had to make the best of it.

But seeing Sam had really thrown her for a loop.
By the time she had fallen into bed the night be-

fore, she was so dazed that she accepted what she was doing. Now, in the harsh light of morning, the full reality of it hit her right in the face. She had committed the worst-possible crime against a friend—not just any friend, but Sam.

"I am *not* looking forward to this day," she muttered as she opened the closet door. Deliberately choosing her least attractive clothes, a pair of baggy jeans and a shapeless gray sweatshirt, she slowly got dressed. Then she moped around the suite for a while, wishing time would pass more swiftly so she could go to class, turn in her paper, and get the whole thing over with.

When it was time to leave, Maddie forced herself to wait a few extra minutes. She wanted to give Sam plenty of time to get to class. Then she could go in just before Professor Harrison and get a seat by the door. She didn't think she could ever look Sam in the eye again.

"As you leave, you will see boxes on the table outside the door with your section leaders' names on them. Please put your paper in the appropriate box. Thank you." With a nod, Professor Harrison tapped his notes together to signal that the lecture was over. Immediately he was besieged by students with questions.

Maddie slipped out of her seat at the back of the auditorium and pushed through the door ahead of the throng. At the table she paused, holding her paper just above her section leader's box. She hesitated, in a turmoil of indecision and confusing, conflicting emotions. There was still time to change her mind, time to back out. But at that moment somebody bumped her elbow, and she dropped the paper in the box. It was done. Turning quickly, she hurried to the outside door.

As she ran down the steps, she heard Sam's voice calling out to her. "Maddie! Hey, Maddie! Wait up!" But she pretended not to hear and quickened her pace, her head lowered. There was no way she could face Sam and pretend everything was fine. She was sure that if she had to talk to Sam, she would blurt out the whole, miserable story. And that would mean disaster.

What she needed was to go somewhere quiet, where she could be alone to collect her thoughts. The theater immediately sprang to mind: it was dark, hushed, isolated. In midstride she changed direction and headed for the Fine Arts Complex. Soon she was jogging up the carpeted steps to the theater, which was usually deserted at this time of the day. With a feeling of relief, she yanked open the door and stepped inside.

Onstage, the sets for *A Midsummer Night's Dream* stood around in a state of semicompletion, and an empty pizza carton perched on top of a tool chest. A few dim lights were on, sending a faint glow out into the house. Maddie sank gratefully onto a seat and leaned her head back.

She sat that way for several minutes, trying to clear her mind. She just couldn't let herself think about it—it was too awful. If she looked closely at herself, she knew she would see something ugly, so she just concentrated on the ceiling. After a while a sort of dull, resigned peace came over her, and she drew a deep breath. All of a sudden she heard the backstage door opening, and she panicked, hoping desperately that no one would find her.

Steps resounded woodenly on the stage, paused, and came closer. Maddie looked carefully over near the wings—it was Stu! She couldn't believe her bad luck. He was bending down, carefully checking the painted flats and platforms. His sandy blond hair fell forward across his eyes and reflected the light above him. Maddie's heart began to pound, and she wondered frantically if she was going to start crying. Because she knew right at that moment that she couldn't go on seeing Stu with this on her conscience. She would always feel like a liar, always hiding the truth about herself and never being honest with him. A sob welled up in her throat, and she clamped a shaking hand over her mouth.

He stood up abruptly and squinted out into the darkness. "Is somebody here?" he called out uncertainly, shading his eyes with one hand.

Maddie shrank back into the plush fabric of her seat, praying he wouldn't see her. She would give anything to avoid confronting him right now.

Stooping down, he picked up an industrial-size flashlight and switched it on. Maddie closed her eyes and felt the strong beam of light flash across her face.

"Maddie?"

"Yeah, it's me," she said defeatedly. With a sigh of resignation, she pulled herself to her feet and dragged herself down the aisle toward him.

"Well, what were you hiding for?' Stu hitched himself up onto a sawhorse and watched her climb onto the stage. "Were you spying on me or something?" His voice was teasing, and a smile played around the corners of his mouth.

"No, just thinking," she said tonelessly, fighting to keep a tremble from her voice.

"Hmm ... I think this is very suspicious," he continued, rubbing his chin thoughtfully as he looked at her. "Maybe you should elaborate on that a little bit."

Unable to return his playful smile, Maddie dropped her books onto a crate and leaned back against the sawhorse, staring at her feet. She shrugged. "I don't know. It's nothing."

He touched her shoulder lightly. "Hey, something's wrong. What is it?"

Speechless, she shook her head.

"Want to talk about it?"

The tenderness in his voice was too much for her, and without warning Maddie burst into tears. She pressed her fist to her mouth and squeezed her eyes shut tightly as deep sobs shook her body.

"Maddie! Maddie, what is it?" Distressed, Stu put his arms awkwardly around her and patted the top of her head. "Hey, calm down, huh?"

For a moment all she could do was let out the built-up tension from the night before. Then, as suddenly as she had started crying, she stopped. Sniffing miserably, she sat up and pulled away from Stu, wiping the tears off her face. She couldn't bring herself to look at him.

"Want to talk about it?"

"No."

"Maddie, I don't understand! Something is obviously bothering you, and I'd like to help if I can."

She shook her head emphatically and turned away from him. Fixing her eyes on a hammer that was lying on the floor, she concentrated on keeping herself under control. More than anything else, she wished she could unburden herself to Stu, rest her head on his warm shoulder and let him comfort her. But what would he think of her if she told him what she had done? She could never be honest with him now, and that meant breaking off their relationship for good.

Next to her, she could feel Stu's presence, as well as the friction that had sprung up between them. Obviously he was hurt that she wouldn't confide in him.

He sighed. "I wish you could trust me," he said, echoing her thoughts.

"It's nothing, okay?" she snapped, jumping up quickly and walking several paces away to the edge of the stage. She had a fleeting impression of the two of them carrying on this awkward scene on the cluttered stage like actors in a modern drama. "I woke up with a headache, and I feel rotten. That's all it is."

"Well, I'm sorry I asked. You don't have to be offended just because I was concerned about you! I was only trying to help, you know."

"Well, I don't need any help, okay?" she snapped.

There was an ominous silence, and Maddie

closed her eyes. I have really blown it, she thought wretchedly. If he thinks I'm a total jerk, he's right.

Stu let his breath out slowly, and the sawhorse scraped sharply on the floor as he pushed himself away from it. For a moment Maddie was afraid he was going to walk toward her, and she held her breath. But instead he turned and walked offstage. A few seconds later, the door slammed shut, and Maddie was alone in the theater. Alone with her conscience.

Chapter 11

After lunch on Friday, Maddie took a roundabout route back to her dorm, dawdling along the paths and trying to enjoy the spring tulips and hyacinths that lit up the well-kept flower beds with vibrant color. She had passed a restless night, but she was resolved to put the Shakespeare episode behind her—what was done was done. The only thing to do was make the best of it and never let it happen again. Of course, what that meant was she had to start doing the rest of her work right away. But for the moment she just wanted to breathe in the moist, balmy air and the delicate scent of the magnolias.

"Maddie, hold on!"

She turned and saw Roni jogging toward her, a half-eaten apple in her hand. Roni fell into step

beside her, and they continued walking toward
Rogers House.

"Spring barbecue's tomorrow—did you see the
announcement?" Roni asked through a juicy
mouthful of apple. "First campus picnic of the year.
Should be great."

Maddie nodded absently and kicked at a pebble.
"Yeah, it sounds like fun," she mumbled, and dug
her hands into her pockets, her thoughts far away.

"Fun? Girl, you don't know what you're talking
about," Roni crowed. She took Maddie's arm and
waved her apple core in front of them as though
gesturing toward a crowded picnic lawn.

"Having a barbecue is a religious experience in
the South, you know. Ever since way back before
the days of Scarlett O'Hara, we Georgians have
been licking our fingers and smacking our lips over
the barbecue pits. Ribs, Jell-O salad, tons of gooey,
sugary-sweet things. Ooh!" Roni heaved a blissful
sigh. "And there's going to be a great blue-grass
band—the Good Old Boys. They'll have the whole
campus jumping in two minutes. Guaranteed."

They walked a few more steps without speaking. Roni seemed to be waiting for some kind of
enthusiastic reaction from Maddie and kept darting
her looks from between her lashes. But Maddie
couldn't bring herself to respond. She didn't care
about the barbecue. There was no way she was
going to have a good time, and she didn't feel like
watching everyone else's.

"Hello in there!" Roni yelled.

Maddie laughed in spite of herself. "Sorry. I was
just thinking, that's all."

"Oh, no, don't do that."

With a wry grin, Maddie pushed open the front door of the dorm and stepped inside. Roni stopped to check the mailboxes while Maddie waited by the stairs.

"Maddie, is that you? Hey, I'm glad I caught you."

Turning quickly, Maddie found Pam, the resident adviser, leaning out over the stairs from the landing above. "Hi, Pam. What is it?"

Pam tucked a lock of red hair behind one ear. "I got a call on my campus phone from the English department secretary—she didn't have your phone number."

Maddie's heart skipped a beat, then began thudding rapidly as she looked up the stairwell at Pam. "Yeah?" she asked guardedly, trying not to shake.

"She said Professor Harrison would like to see you in his office this afternoon at two o'clock. If you can make it then. If you can't, call and let her know."

Maddie felt as if she had been struck by a thunderbolt or as if someone had just punched her below the ribs: she could barely breathe for a few seconds. But she forced herself to give Pam a nonchalant, carefree smile while the ground opened up beneath her feet. "Okay. Thanks."

"Sure. No problem. See you later!" Pam's head popped out of sight again over the banister.

Roni walked back slowly toward the stairs, shuffling through a stack of letters and leaflets. As she reached the bottom step she looked up at Maddie with a smile. Maddie stared back at her without saying anything. Breathing shallowly through her mouth, she pressed her trembling hands against her sides.

"Hey, you look like you just ate a worm."

With an effort, Maddie shook off her growing feeling of panic and tried to look normal. "It's nothing," she said hollowly, glancing quickly at her watch. It was one-thirty. "I just remembered something I have to do, that's all."

"Okay. Are you coming upstairs?" Roni put her hand on the banister and cocked her head to one side. "Oh Maaaa-die. Earth to Maddie."

"No. No—I'll see you later. Bye."

Maddie turned and went out the door, walking as if she'd been hypnotized. Maybe Professor Harrison had something totally unrelated to discuss with her, she thought wildly. There's no way he could know about the paper. No possible way.

She stepped out into the brilliant sunshine, and immediately a cloud drifted across the sun. Maddie shivered and fought off the superstitious feeling that it was a bad omen. She put her head down and struck out across the campus.

In a few minutes she was hurrying up the steps of the faculty office building, and she turned down an echoing, marble-tiled corridor toward the English department. "Which is Professor Harrison's office?" she asked breathlessly as she approached the department secretary's desk.

The woman looked up briefly from her work. "Number one seventeen. Down the hall to the right."

Maddie turned down the hallway, walking as

stiffly as a sleepwalker. Posters for foreign-exchange study programs dotted the walls: the battlement towers and Gothic arches of a dozen European universities appeared one after the other as Maddie strode down the hall. On other trips here she had paused to linger over these notices, drinking in the alluring flavor of those ancient institutions of learning. But this time she didn't even see them. Her eyes only darted from side to side to count off the office numbers until she reached number one seventeen. The closed door bore an engraved brass nameplate: Stanley Harrison.

She stopped herself just in time as she raised her hand to knock. It was only one forty-five. But suddenly the door swung open and Professor Harrison appeared on the threshold. "Can I help you?"

She jumped guiltily. "Yes. I'm—Madison Lerner," she croaked through dry lips.

"Come in, please." He stepped aside to usher her into his book-lined office. Her heart pounding unevenly, Maddie walked in and sat gingerly on the edge of a cracked-leather chair. He followed her, closing the door behind him, and sat down at the desk, which was piled high with books and papers.

There was a deadly silence as Maddie waited for him to speak. He leaned back in his chair and pressed his fingertips together. Then he looked at her intently from underneath his bushy eyebrows for what seemed like a lifetime.

"Your section leader is Ms. Walsh, is that right?"
She nodded silently.

"And did you know that Ms. Walsh is married to Mr. Morrisey?"

Maddie's heart turned over sickeningly. Mr. Morrisey was Sam's section leader. Unable to speak, she nodded for the professor continue.

"Ms. Walsh and Mr. Morrisey often exchange papers to read," he said, giving her another piercing look. "It may interest you to know that they found your paper and another to be quite similar—different wording, of course, but to all intents and purposes, virtually identical. Have you any comment to make about this?"

"No." Maddie knew her voice was barely audible, and she felt her face turning ashy white. Sweat broke out on her palms, and she noiselessly rubbed her hands on her skirt.

"I see." Professor Harrison nodded and sat forward to consult some papers on his desk. "Do you know that Hawthorne College has such a thing as an honor board? Do you know what that is?" he asked, sitting back again.

She nodded and tried her hardest to swallow the lump in her throat.

"The honor board receives reports of suspected academic misconduct at this college, and makes determinations about their validity. In other words, they are a court of academic law." His face was turned to the window, and he tapped a pencil on his desk. "It is my obligation to inform the honor board of violations, Miss Lerner."

"I—I—"

"Yes?" He swung around quickly to look at her. "Would you like to say something?"

A picture came to Maddie's mind of a row of judges looking down from a high bench. Their fingers pointed at her accusingly, and the spokesman pronounced her sentence: EXPELLED.

She cleared her throat painfully and stared into his dark, intense eyes. She felt like a mouse staring at an approaching rattlesnake. "No. I don't have anything to say."

His mouth twisted with irritation, and he drew his eyebrows together menacingly. "I have no way of determining which of the two papers is authentic, and which one is plagiarized."

Maddie winced involuntarily at the word.

"I will not, of course, tell you the name of the other student involved, nor will I inform that student of your identity."

I already know, Maddie said silently, her eyes stinging with tears.

"You and the other student will have until one week from today to come forward with the truth. If, at that time, neither of you has claimed responsibility, I will report this to the honor board and give both of you a failing grade. That is all."

Maddie rose mechanically to her feet and made her way to the door. She pulled it shut behind her and stood staring at the opposite wall. It felt as if the world were caving in around her, and there was nothing she could do to hold it back.

Sam would find out, too. That was inevitable, wasn't it? Professor Harrison would be giving her the same ultimatum. Maddie's heart turned over with a painful thump, and tears began spilling out over her cheeks. She put her hands up to her burning face and shook her head in total despair. If only she could just go back in time and undo what she'd done! It was a nightmare, an absolute nightmare. And there was no waking up from this one.

After three hours of wandering aimlessly around campus, Maddie paused with her hand on the door knob of suite 2C. Briefly she closed her eyes, then nodded, took a deep breath, and opened the door with a big smile on her face. No matter what, she had to keep up appearances—she couldn't let anyone know she was falling apart inside.

But when she opened the door, her smile vanished. Sam was on the couch, sniffling into a crumpled tissue. Next to her, Stacy was rubbing Sam's neck and telling her everything would be all right. Roni was seated on the floor, leaning forward with her elbows on her knees, staring glumly at Sam.

Maddie caught her breath. "Wh—what's going on?" she stammered, her eyes darting between the other three girls.

At the sound of her voice, Sam shifted around on the couch to look at her, her face streaked with tears. "Oh, Maddie! Something terrible has happened! I don't know what I'm going to do!" Her control dissolved, and tears welled up and over her matted eyelashes.

"Some jerk copied Sam's paper for Shakespeare class, and Sam's going to flunk the class unless they confess," Roni stormed, stamping to her feet and pulling the window curtain aside angrily. She glared at the balcony railing, her jaw clenched. "She might even be expelled! Can you imagine?

Some people are such slimes. It really makes me sick."

"I don't know what I'm going to do!" Sam wailed again, shaking her head in despair. "If I fail that class, I won't make Phi Beta Kappa—I might not be able to major in English anymore!" She wiped futilely at her eyes with a wet, crumpled tissue. It fell apart in her hands, and she flung it down in disgust. "And if I have to go to the honor board ..." Another pitiful sob wrenched through her.

"Here." Calmly, Stacy handed her another tissue and shook her head. "We've just got to figure out who did this to you, that's all."

Her hands shaking, Maddie pulled out a chair and sat down. In her panic, wondering desperately what she was going to do, it had slipped her mind that the professor would be talking to Sam, too. With her guilty conscience, it seemed natural that he would only tell *her*. But of course Sam had been given the same sentence: confess or flunk.

As for Sam, she was obviously in shock. Through absolutely no fault of her own, she had been told she might fail one of her most important classes. Maddie knew in her heart that Sam would never even consider cheating, so of course it would be hard for Sam to believe that other people actually did. Her cheeks were pale and streaked with tears, and she kept covering her eyes with her hand, as though trying to make a horrible vision disappear.

At the window, Roni swore under her breath, and Maddie felt her stomach turn over. Roni was talking about *her* and didn't even realize it. Maddie

didn't think she could bear it if Roni and Stacy—
and worst of all, Sam—knew she was the "slime"
who had done this. She clenched her hands together in her lap and said nothing.

"I just don't understand how it could have happened, though," Sam said, catching her breath as
she tried to bring her tears under control. "I mean,
how could someone have copied it without my
knowing?"

"Well, did you ever leave it anywhere?" Roni
asked. She threw herself into a chair and looked
intently into Sam's face. Sam shook her head in
bewilderment. "Not even for a little while?"

"No. Well—wait a minute." Sam's voice changed
slightly, and she sat up a little straighter on the
couch, her forehead creased with concentration.

"Well?" Stacy prompted.

"I was working on the final draft earlier in the
week in a carrel in the library," Sam said slowly.
"I remember recognizing a lot of people from my
Shakespeare class, and thinking they were probably all working on their papers. And at one point
I went out to the lounge to get a candy bar from
one of the vending machines."

Roni nodded eagerly. "How long were you
gone? Ten minutes? Five minutes? What?"

"Well, I ran into a friend from one of my classes
last semester, and we started talking...." Sam
shook her head and made a sour face. "I don't
know—it might have been twenty minutes or even
more. I really don't remember."

As if in a dream, Maddie heard herself say,

"There are copying machines on every floor in the library, you know."

Sam turned around quickly, an angry fire kindling in her usually gentle brown eyes. "That's *right!* Someone could have copied the rough draft right there—it would only have taken a couple of minutes."

"That must be it, then." Roni sighed, then pressed her lips together and shook her head. "Can you believe what disgusting things some people will do? It's so totally beneath contempt."

The impassioned sparkle faded from Sam's eyes, and her shoulders slumped with defeat. "Sure. But that doesn't help me very much, does it? I mean, I still don't know who it was, and there's no way of knowing whether they'll take the blame or not. So far, he or she doesn't seem like the type to do *that.*"

Maddie stared at the floor, her cheeks burning with mortification. Better never to say anything than to have them turn their contempt and outrage on her. The professor would just flunk them both, she told herself desperately. He probably wouldn't actually go to the honor board. Facing the honor board for this could easily mean expulsion, and she couldn't allow herself to think about that. No, definitely the best she could hope for was the professor just giving them F's. She could always take five courses again one semester to make up the credit.

And she'd make it up to Sam somehow—*somehow.* But she couldn't admit it now. They would never, never forgive her. The thought of losing the new friendships that meant so much to her made her physically sick. *She just couldn't do it.*

And if she denied it consistently to her professor, and to her parents, nobody could *prove* she was lying. She would have to take a failing grade, but she could turn the story around so that at least her parents would never know it was her fault. And since grade reports didn't come out until after the semester was over and everyone had left school, there was no way Sam would ever find out she'd failed Shakespeare.

"Oh, Sam, I'm so sorry!" she whispered, her chin quivering dangerously.

Sam lifted her head and smiled bravely. "Oh, Maddie, you must think I'm such an idiot, leaving my paper around so carelessly."

Shamed into utter speechlessness, Maddie shook her head. She didn't know how much longer she could stay in the same room with her suitemates. Little tremors began to shake her, and she made herself go rigid as she grappled for control.

"Well, I don't," Roni snorted. "I mean, you'd have to be totally paranoid to suspect everyone you see of wanting to cheat off you. There's no way you could have known this would happen, Sam, so don't act like you are in any way to blame."

"That's right," Stacy put in, putting a hand on Sam's shoulder and looking her in the eye. "Don't blame yourself. You wrote an excellent paper— whoever did this had good sense, at least."

Sam laughed ruefully and put a hand up to her

mouth as the chuckle threatened to turn into a sob. "Yeah, I guess I should be flattered, huh?"

The phone rang, and Roni leaned over to pick it up. "Hello? Well, yeah, she's right here, hang on a sec."

Covering the mouthpiece with one hand, she nodded at Maddie. "It's for you—it's Stu."

"No!" Maddie shook her head emphatically and backed away. "I really can't talk to him right now," she pleaded, defensively crossing her arms across her chest. "I really don't want to. It's a bad time."

Roni shrugged and spoke into the phone again. "Stu, she's kind of tied up at the moment. Do you want to call back later?" Maddie shook her head again, her eyes wide with alarm. "Or she'll call you, how's that? Okay? Bye—yeah. Bye."

"Oh, Maddie," Sam cried as Roni hung up the telephone, "you didn't have to do that—I'm not going to fall to pieces." She smiled tenderly over the back of the couch. "You're so sweet to do that, but you could have talked to him. Really."

Maddie's eyes widened even further as she met Sam's grateful smile. Sam thought she had turned Stu down out of concern for her—because if their positions had been reversed, that was exactly what Sam would have done. She had to be one of the most innocent, unsuspecting people in the world. Rather than zero in on the most likely person to have copied her paper—the one who lived in the same suite—she was ready to suspect anybody else. According to Sam, friendship made certain assumptions: one of them was that friends didn't copy each other's Shakespeare papers.

With a dejected sigh, Samantha sat back on the couch and smiled sadly at her suitemates. "I can't believe this happened, but I'm sure it will clear up. It has to," she added fiercely. Then she smiled again through her tears. "And I am so glad you guys are my friends. You make disasters a lot easier to cope with."

"Oh, Sam!" Stacy leaned over and wrapped Sam in a big bear hug, and Roni bounced over and put her arms around them both.

Without a word, Maddie pushed herself to her feet and walked into the bathroom. She turned the lock quietly. For a moment, she stood with her back to the door, staring at her pale, hollow-eyed reflection in the mirror. Then she sat down on the edge of the bathtub and buried her head in her arms as tears of shame and anxiety welled up and spilled out over her cheeks. "What have I done?" she whispered in anguish. "What have I done?"

Chapter 12

Maddie lifted her eyes briefly from her Greek history book as Sam came into the living room and slumped down a little lower on the couch. She wished she was invisible. Every waking moment in the suite was unbearable, but the worst thing was that Sam kept seeking her out—for support and comfort.

"Hi, Maddie." With a heavy sigh, Sam dropped into a chair and sat staring gloomily out the window. "I don't feel very much like going to this barbecue today, I really don't."

Me neither, Maddie agreed silently. For a moment her eyes strayed to the open window: outside, a glorious spring morning was unfolding. There wasn't a cloud in the sky, and a warm breeze moved the curtains gently. It would be a perfect day for a picnic. She could just imagine how the athletic fields would look in an hour, covered with blankets and bodies soaking up the hot sun.

But she turned back resolutely to her book again. From now on, she had to devote all her time to her studies. No more racing around trying to do everything. It seemed like it was either one or the other with her: either she did everything or nothing. Well, it would have to be nothing, she told herself as she set her mouth in a grim line. She couldn't afford to make any more mistakes. And anyway, she couldn't possibly get any enjoyment out of a picnic now—especially not if Sam was going.

"Are we all ready to eat ten tons of barbecued spare ribs today?" Roni chirped, strolling in from her bedroom as she struggled with the buttons on the back of a sleeveless blouse. She smiled broadly at them both and took a deep breath of fresh air. "What a day, huh? Purr-fect."

Neither Maddie nor Sam said anything.

"Boy, you two are really just a barrel of laughs today, let me tell you." Roni quirked one eyebrow at them and shook her head. "Listen, there's no point in moping around, Sam. You can't let this thing get to you."

"But Roni—" Sam broke off and shook her head. "You just don't understand."

"Sam! Come on, who do you think you're talking to, anyway?"

Sam stared back at Roni bleakly.

"Listen." Roni sat down on the couch next to Maddie and tucked her legs up underneath her.

"We've been through a lot together, Sam. When I was partying my brains out and didn't realize what I was doing, you were there for me. And you were there for Stace when she was heading for anorexia and wouldn't listen to us, right?"

Maddie felt a pang of sadness as she realized her three suitemates had already shared so many experiences together. They had a special bond. And she had wrecked her chances of joining that special relationship; it was way too late for that now.

Roni and Sam were looking at each other seriously, and then Sam smiled ruefully. "I guess we've all been through the mill this year, huh?"

"You're darn right," Roni retorted with a toss of her head. "So think twice before you say we don't understand what you're going through, okay? Okay?" she repeated, frowning at Sam with mock ferocity.

"Okay!" Sam chuckled and rested her chin in her hand. "I guess I'm just feeling sorry for myself, that's all. The thought of being expelled for something I didn't do—" Her voice cracked, and she swallowed hard. There was a heavy silence in the room. Off in the distance, they could hear the erratic twanging of amplified electric guitars tuning up.

"But hey," she said brightly, "I'm not going to let this get me down. I really believe that whoever did it will finally confess."

Maddie felt her cheeks get hot, and she lowered her head farther to look at her book. The words and photographs on the page turned into a blur. Roni leaned over and gave Sam a playful punch on the knee. "That's the spirit. Now how about getting our act together and going to this barbecue, huh?"

"Okay, okay, you win." Sam poised to rise from her chair and looked inquiringly at Maddie. "You're coming, aren't you, Mad?"

"I—I don't think I should—I have a lot of studying to do," she stammered, not daring to meet Sam's eyes.

"Maddie! Come on! You're carrying this good student act a little too far, don't you think?" Roni teased with an incredulous smile. "Besides, this is what you keep telling us you wanted to move onto campus for, right? To get a good social life? Of course, some of us already have that," Roni said as she flipped her auburn hair over her shoulder.

Maddie looked in confusion from Roni to Sam and back again. They were so eager to have her go—she couldn't believe it. But of course they didn't know the truth about her. They still thought of her as an honest friend.

"I don't know," she repeated. "I really do have a lot of work." She waved vaguely in the direction of her room. She couldn't even think what classes she had, she was so flustered and confused about what to do.

Before Maddie knew what was happening, Roni had jumped up and dragged her by the arm to their bedroom. "Maddie! I honestly cannot believe you!" Roni admonished as she closed the door and faced her. "Sam is so upset about this stupid paper business. Don't you think you could help me and Stace try to cheer her up? It's only for a few hours."

"I know, but—"

"Maddie, please! I know it's hard for you to imagine being on the verge of total academic collapse, but try to understand how Sam must feel."

Maddie dropped her eyes. "I know," she whispered. "I do understand."

"Then you'll come?"

Maddie swallowed. "Yes." She sighed heavily. "When you put it like that—of course I will."

"Great." Roni took Maddie in tow again, and they returned to the living room.

Sam looked up with a sad smile. "You should only come if you really want to, Maddie. It won't be the same without you there, but you really don't have to do it for my sake."

As Maddie met Sam's warm, earnest gaze, she couldn't help smiling back. More than anything else, Sam's friendship was what had made moving into suite 2C so great. Firmly putting the impending disaster out of her mind, Maddie nodded. If Sam wanted her to go, she'd go. "Okay, Sam. I'll come."

"I'm a lone cowha-a-a-nd, from the Rio Gra-a-a-ande. But my legs ain't bow-w-w-wed, and my cheeks ain't ta-a-an. I'm a cowboy who never saw a cow, never roped a steer 'cause I don't know how, and I sure ain't fixin' to start it now. Yippy-ai-o kiyay!"

Roni and Stacy giggled hysterically as they sang along with the Good Old Boys blue-grass band and danced barefoot together on the grass. The slide guitar vibrated mellowly from the gigantic sound system, and the handsome lead singer crooned directly into the microphone, giving the girls up front a seductive smile. All around, hundreds of Hawthorne students were milling about, talking, dancing, and singing or carrying heaping plates of food from the long tables by the barbecue pits.

"Come on, Sam, how about a dance, huh?" Aaron propped himself up on his elbow on the big blanket and caressed Sam's arm. He gave her a disarming smile as he looked up at her.

She smiled but shook her head. "I don't really feel like it."

He looked at her sadly for a moment and shook his head. "I understand. How about you, then, Maddie?" he asked, leaning his head back to look at her. She was sitting on the very corner of the blanket, trying to be invisible.

Startled, Maddie turned to meet his eyes. "Oh, not me," she said, blushing. "I'm, uh, too hungry." She picked up a half-eaten chicken wing and began nibbling on it. She was beginning to think she had made a big mistake coming. Everyone was having such a good time, and she felt even more like an outsider than she had before she'd moved onto campus. Keeping her eyes down, she licked the spicy-sweet barbecue sauce off her fingers.

"Well, if nobody wants to dance with me, I'm going to go see if I can get up a game of Frisbee golf," Aaron announced, scrambling to his feet. "Last chance," he said, looking down at Sam with a tender smile.

"No—go on, Aaron. I'm just going to stay here and listen to the music, okay?"

He shrugged. "Okay. See you later." With a

mock salute, he turned and jogged off to join Zack and Pete at the far end of the athletic fields, where Frisbees were already spinning through the air.

Maddie watched him go, and her gaze traveled across the crowd, idly searching. She was looking for Stu, even though she didn't want to admit it to herself. After their argument on Thursday, she had pretty much decided that whatever they had together, as a couple, was over. He couldn't possibly think she was worth any more of his time. She had been so rude to him on the stage and then never called him back to apologize. Besides, she didn't deserve to have someone like him.

But she couldn't help looking for him anyway. A gap suddenly opened in a big group of people, and she caught a glimpse of a head of sandy blond hair near the barbecue pit. Her heart skipped a beat. But when the boy turned around, it was someone else, and he leaned down to whisper in a cute girl's ear. Sighing heavily, Maddie poked at her coleslaw with a plastic fork, pushing it around the plate. Her appetite had completely vanished.

"Maddie, just because I'm being such a downer doesn't mean you can't have a good time, you know," said Sam.

Maddie looked up quickly into Sam's eyes, then dropped her gaze. "I'm not really in a partying mood, I guess. Don't mind me."

"You could have danced with Aaron—I really wouldn't mind."

Staring down at the blanket, Maddie shook her head. She picked carefully at a few blades of grass, wishing she could find the right words to say. "No," she said hoarsely. "I just didn't want to dance. Honest." Her voice faded out on the last word. She pushed herself up off the blanket. "I'll be back in a minute," she explained quickly. Then she hurried through the crowd of students, not even knowing where she was going.

Her wandering steps brought her to the fieldhouse. She rounded the corner of the building and leaned back against the bricks, gasping for breath and grateful for the shade.

A twig cracked, and she turned quickly. Stu was right behind her.

"Hi," he said, a hesitant smile on his face. "I saw you coming this way. I've been trying to call to you." He gestured back toward the picnic area. "I thought we could eat together."

Maddie was overcome with emotion, and she shook her head without a word.

Stu's smile faded into an apologetic frown, and he took a step forward. "Hey, about the other day when I was so rude—I'm really sorry. I shouldn't have acted like such a jerk because you didn't want to talk. Whatever was bothering you was none of my business, so I'm sorry."

She still couldn't speak, and he looked at her quizzically. "Still friends? Maddie, did you hear me? I'm sorry."

"Stu," she heard herself say through a fog. "Stu, I can't work on the play with you anymore."

His eyes widened with surprise. "What—?"

She had to keep talking, or she wouldn't be able to go through with it. She had to make it perfectly clear that she didn't want to see him anymore—

because seeing him now was torture to her, knowing that she had thrown their relationship away—for a stupid paper. Moving a few steps away, she spoke in a low, controlled voice. "I just realized I don't have the time to spend on extra projects. I'm sorry, that's just the way it is. I have to go now."

"Maddie! Wait!"

Briefly she turned and met his eyes, but the hurt and confusion she saw in his face tore at her heart. Gritting her teeth, she turned and ran back toward the picnic lawn.

"Whew!" Stacy gasped, dropping down onto the blanket beside them. She tucked her skirt around her knees and reached over for Maddie's untouched soda. She drank deeply and lowered the can with a beaming smile. "Roni is still going strong. I guess you have to be born in the South to dance this long. I don't know how she does it, but I am totally exhausted."

Stretching luxuriously, Stacy lifted her glossy blond hair off her neck and turned her face up to the sun. "This is great. And I've eaten two drumsticks, if you can believe it," she added, turning to look at Sam.

"That's great, Stacy," Sam said, giving her friend an encouraging nod. "It must be pretty hard to come to a picnic, huh?"

Stacy pursed her lips thoughtfully as she considered it. "It's not as bad as I thought it would be," she admitted slowly. "I mean, we talk a lot in the eating disorders group about things like this—going out to restaurants, parties, you know." She met Maddie's puzzled look and gave her a lopsided grin. "I'm kind of anorexic, didn't you know?"

Shaking her head, Maddie said, "Not until Roni mentioned it this morning. I had no idea. You seem to eat pretty normally."

"Well . . ." Stacy shrugged matter-of-factly. "I've got it pretty well under control. Thanks to Sam and Roni."

"You did it yourself, Stacy," Sam said modestly. As Stacy shook her head she added, "Yes, you did, and you know it. You had to do it on your own in the end."

"Well, I couldn't have done it without you, no matter what you say," Stacy insisted, lying back on her elbows and crossing her slim ankles. She turned to Maddie. "You don't know what those two went through with me. And I'll never forget them for it."

"Forgive us, you mean." Sam laughed and pushed Stacy over on to her side. Stacy yelped.

Maddie smiled faintly at her friends, her thoughts spinning. *Am I really doing this to her?* she asked herself in disbelief. *Whatever happened to all my standards and values?* She remembered her reaction when her suitemates suggested that shopping trip to Atlanta. She had been horrified to think they were so willing to cut classes. And here she was, a traitor and a cheat, sitting next to Sam and Stacy, knowing full well that she would be the cause of the biggest disaster in Sam's life. And that she wasn't planning to do anything about it.

"Sam, I—"

"Get *up*, you lazy slugs, and dance!" With typical drama, Roni jumped into their midst, sending paper plates flying. "This is no way to act at a picnic. I am truly ashamed of you all."

Maddie caught her breath and let it out slowly. Roni had stopped her just in time. Confessing would only mean disgrace and failure, and she just didn't think she could go through that. All her life she had been the star pupil, the apple of her parents' eyes, fulfilling all their expectations. She could picture with painful clarity their expressions of horror, hurt, and disappointment if she told them she had plagiarized a Shakespeare paper.

"Okay," laughed Sam as Roni pulled her forcefully to her feet. "I'll dance. But only if Maddie does."

Roni turned to Maddie with a determined look. "This is it, Lerner. You can sit there and completely *ruin* Sam's day, or get up and help us party."

For a moment Maddie stared into Roni's twinkling eyes. It was too ironic. What with breaking up with Stu, and faking her way through the barbecue, it was turning out to be an unbelievably painful afternoon. And now Roni was telling her not to ruin Sam's day! Maddie seriously wondered how much longer she could keep it up. With a grim sigh of determination, she clambered to her feet. Anything she could do to help Sam, she would. Anything except confess.

By Monday the only thing that was clear to Maddie was that she couldn't make time stand still, no matter how much she wished she could. Professor Harrison expected some kind of answer on Thursday, but Maddie kept thinking that something was bound to come up, that there had to be some way to get out of it. There just *had* to be. Of course, what that was, she couldn't imagine.

In Shakespeare, she stared sightlessly into space, shaking her head over her stupidity. It was her own fault she was in this mess, there was no question about that. By trying to do everything there was to do, she had royally blown it. I'll just quit everything, that's all, she decided at last. The first thing she'd do was cancel her afternoon tour. She headed for the admissions office right after class.

"Hi—it's Maddie, isn't it?" Mrs. Neale, the admissions secretary, said with a bright smile. "I've heard good things about you already. You're going to make an excellent guide."

Maddie dropped her eyes in embarrassment to the blue pile rug. "Oh, well—I hate to say this, but I can't do it after all. I—I have to spend more time on my schoolwork."

"Oh. Oh, I see." Mrs. Neale sighed audibly. "Well, I guess I can get someone else for this afternoon. You're sure you won't change your mind?"

Shaking her head firmly, Maddie whispered, "No. I'm sorry. I can't." With a regretful wave, she turned and walked purposefully out of the building.

"Maddie!"

She turned slowly and saw Holly running to catch up with her. Before her friend could speak, she said in a rush, "Holly, I won't be coming to watch *GH* anymore—I decided I'm too busy. And I can't go to that recital with you, either."

Holly looked at her in surprise. "What—?"

"I'm sorry, Holly. I have to go." Without meeting her friend's eyes, she turned and walked away. Holly was only the first person she was going to have to break a date with, Maddie realized sadly. She had made dates and arrangements for the whole week and a lot for the following week, too. And now she would have to cancel every single one of them. It would be hard, but she just had to do it.

The hardest thing of all, though, was trying to keep up her act around her friends. Every time she entered the suite, she felt like a spy—hiding her true identity under a mask of concern and friendship. And the tension in suite 2C had become unbearable. Stacy and Roni walked around on tiptoe, and Sam spent more and more time staring blankly into space instead of studying. She was waiting for Thursday, too. Maybe even more anxiously. Maddie watched and waited in silent agony and kept praying hopelessly for a miracle.

On Wednesday afternoon, Maddie was sitting on her bed, trying to concentrate on her macroeconomics notes. There was a gentle knock, and Sam poked her head in the door. "Knock, knock."

Maddie closed her notebook hesitantly. "Hi," she said quietly, trying to swallow. She looked around, hoping there was some excuse to keep Sam out.

Sighing, Sam came in and sat down on the edge of Maddie's bed. She scratched with one finger at a small stain on the bedspread, keeping her eyes down. Her cheeks were flushed unnaturally. "Do you want to come with me to the Dixie Diner?" she asked in a small voice.

There was an awkward pause, and Maddie cursed herself for being such a traitor. But she couldn't say no to Sam about anything now. She felt too guilty not to do whatever Sam wanted. "Sure."

Reluctantly pushing herself off the bed, Maddie walked to the desk to get her wallet and opened the door. Without speaking, they left the suite, walked downstairs, and headed across campus to take the walking path to town. The Dixie Diner was a familiar, cozy place with worn Formica tables and individual jukeboxes in the booths. They reached the diner in a few minutes and slid into two cracked-vinyl seats.

"What'll you have, girls?" the waitress said as she pulled the stub of a pencil from behind her ear.

"Coffee, please. And a raised doughnut," Sam said, her voice low and even.

The waitress shifted her gaze to Maddie, who blushed and nodded. "The same." Maddie reached for the salt shaker, desperate for something to do with her hands. She toyed with it nervously, making little piles of salt on the table.

"So, how are your classes going?" Sam asked with a grim smile as she looked up.

"Fine."

"Did you get your paper back yet?"

The salt shaker dropped with a sharp click, and Maddie busied herself brushing salt over the edge of the table. "No, not yet," she muttered hoarsely.

Sam shrugged and stared out the window. "To-morrow's the deadline," she whispered. "I'm really going to miss this place if I get kicked out." She looked at Maddie again, and her eyes glistened with unshed tears. "I'm really going to miss you too, Maddie."

Maddie felt her chin trembling. She couldn't believe this was happening.

The waitress set down two cups of coffee and two doughnuts and slapped down the check. Sam lifted her cup to her lips and blew on the coffee to cool it. Then, as if it were too heavy to hold, she replaced it with a clatter on the saucer, staring at it blindly. Without warning, she burst into tears.

"Maddie, what am I going to do? My whole life is ruined," she sobbed, her shoulders heaving as she covered her face with her hands. "I just can't believe this is happening to me!"

At that instant, Maddie's resolve broke. She just couldn't go through with this any longer! The sight of Sam crying her heart out across the table from her was more than she could bear. She gripped her hands together tightly in her lap.

"Sam—I—" Her voice cracked, and Sam lifted her tearstained face.

Maddie blinked rapidly trying to hold back her tears. "I did it," she blurted. "I copied your paper. I know you can never forgive me. I've been the worst friend in the entire world."

The look of shock and disbelief on Sam's face was like a knife in Maddie's heart, but she went on breathlessly. "I'll go tell Professor Harrison right now, and then I'll pack my stuff and go back to my aunt's house. I guess I won't be coming back next semester."

For a moment the two girls stared at one another. Sam's mouth moved silently, and her eyes were wide with pain.

Finally, a choking sob escaped from Maddie. "God! I'm so sorry!" She pushed herself out of the booth and ran desperately out of the diner. Another second of Sam's horrified look, and Maddie thought she might die.

Chapter 13

Maddie raced across the road toward campus, oblivious of the squealing tires just behind her as cars slammed on the brakes. There was only one thought in her mind: to get to Professor Harrison and tell him that Sam wasn't guilty.

Heedless of the startled looks of students as she passed, Maddie dashed on, her breath coming in short, harsh gasps. She dodged around pedestrians and made cyclists swerve wildly to avoid hitting her. Her feet pounded up the steps of the faculty office building, and she sped straight-armed through the door. It swung open and banged loudly against the wall.

For a moment Maddie paused to catch her breath in the dark hallway. Her chest heaving, she stood just inside the door, staring wild-eyed up the corridor. A cold wave of fear swept over her as she realized what she was about to do. It could easily mean the end of her college career: no school would accept her as a transfer if she had this on her record. That meant the end of her future plans: no graduate school, no scholarships, *nothing*. But she had to go through with it, for Sam's sake. She could never live with herself if she didn't. She took another deep breath of air to steady herself, then headed resolutely for her professor's office.

She heard the creak of a chair in response to her hurried knock, and heavy footsteps sounded behind the door of room one seventeen. The door opened, and there was Professor Harrison, his face hidden in shadow as light streamed out from a window in the office behind him.

"Miss Lerner," he said matter-of-factly, as thought he were not at all surprised to see her.

Swallowing hard, she nodded. "I'd like to talk to you, if—if it's convenient."

He stepped aside and gestured toward the chair by his desk. Maddie kept her back straight as she walked in ahead of him. She sat, as before, on the very edge of the chair. Now that she was there, all she wanted was to get it over with as soon as possible.

Professor Harrison closed the door and crossed the office to his chair, not speaking as he pulled off his horn-rimmed bifocals and closed a heavy volume on his desk. With the same piercing look, he regarded her with his arms folded across his chest.

Maddie's eyes didn't falter as she met his gaze, but her voice was low as she said, "I was the one who copied the paper, Mr. Harrison. Samantha Hill had nothing to do with it." She paused and swallowed again. "I don't know why I did it, but I did."

Leaning back in his chair, Professor Harrison pursed his lips and scowled thoughtfully. There was a heavy, uncomfortable silence as he continued to look at her with his stern, critical glance.

His chilling reserve began to wear on Maddie, and she felt her face growing hot. "You see, I just moved on campus a few weeks ago, and I got carried away with doing things. I didn't have time to get my paper done. And Sam is my roommate. Her paper was so good. I—I just copied it," she stammered, feeling foolish and weak but unable to stop talking. She knew she wasn't making any sense. If only he would say something!

Finally he nodded and arched one of his bristly, imposing eyebrows. He had never looked quite so intimidating before, and Maddie's heart pounded so hard she was sure he could hear it. "Madison, do you expect me to be sympathetic to you? To understand how you could have let yourself get into such a predicament?"

She stared at him, her eyes burning. "No," she whispered.

"Do you expect clemency from me? A second chance?"

"No." Maddie dropped her eyes, and tried to prepare herself for the inevitable falling of the axe.

"Why not?"

Puzzled, she met his stern gaze again. "I—" She

cleared her throat. "I don't deserve it—I didn't mean to make excuses—just—just to tell you what happened. There *is* no excuse for what I did."

His mouth twisted in a wry, ironic smile. "No, there certainly is not." He turned away and frowned out the window for a few moments. Maddie counted her heartbeats while she waited for him to speak.

"Professor?"

"Hmm?" He swung around again, glowering fiercely at her. "What?"

She drew a shaky breath. "To whom should I report—who on the honor board?"

For a few seconds he looked at her without speaking. Then he leaned forward, resting his elbows on the edge of his desk. "The honor board is likely at best to recommend that you seek a transfer, or at the worst that you be expelled. Do you understand what that means, Miss Lerner?" he exclaimed in a voice as hard as steel.

Holding her breath, Maddie nodded. She prayed she wouldn't start crying and make the situation even worse. "Yes," she said, struggling to hold her voice steady. "I understand."

"You do, eh? Hmm." He frowned again, then seemed to come to a decision. "Miss Lerner, as you know, I have a certain reputation here at this college for being rather—er, implacable, shall we say. But," he continued, his voice softening a bit, "I would not *willingly* see a good student ruin her academic career."

He sat back again, frowning in concentration. His mouth was set in a tight, grim line. Bewildered,

Maddie stared at an ornate jade paperweight on his desk, trying to understand what he meant by that, what he was leading up to. She waited silently for him to go on.

"I'm going to surprise you, Madison." Her eyes flew up to meet his, and he gave her a thin half smile. "I *am* going to grant clemency. I see that you are in shock," he added, his mouth twisting sardonically.

"But—but I—"

"Yes. You cheated, broke the honor code, did many reprehensible things when you copied your roommate's paper," he said with a return to his former severity. "Not the least of them putting a good friend's future at Hawthorne into jeopardy, and using her to make your own life easier."

Maddie swallowed and lowered her head as a hot flush of shame and remorse swept across her face. She nodded in mute agreement and stared at her whitened hands clenched in her lap.

"But I'm fairly confident that this was a one-time aberration on your part. I asked your adviser about your work, and reread your first paper. You are, I feel sure, a good student, and I do not believe you could ever allow yourself to do such a thing again."

"Oh!" Maddie gasped, and shook her head fervently, sending her thick black hair sweeping across her shoulders. "Never again, I swear to God!"

He made a wry grimace. "I'm sure you know what Shakespeare would have said about swearing to the gods. It's a tricky proposition."

For the first time, Maddie saw a light at the end

of the tunnel. She clenched her hands together again to keep them from trembling too noticeably, and a spark of hope kindled in her wide blue eyes. She didn't know what to say anymore, or if she should speak at all. She just nodded.

Professor Harrison pulled a manila folder out from under a pile of scholarly magazines and opened it, scanning quickly over the contents. Then he put it down and looked at her again. "I'm going to offer you a way to make amends, Miss Lerner. Do you know anything about staging a drama—and how that reflects on the message of the play?"

Maddie's mind ran over the dozens and dozens of Shakespeare plays she had seen with her parents: from strictly traditional interpretations to wildly modern and experimental productions. Each new rendering of a Shakespeare drama cast a slightly different light on it. She nodded quickly and licked her dry lips.

"Good. I propose that you study the text of the English department's production of *A Midsummer Night's Dream* and give me an in-depth study of two very different stagings for it. They must both be entirely consistent with the play, historically and dramatically, and they must emphasize two utterly different themes. Do you understand?"

"Yes, yes, I do."

"And I expect it to be no less than thirty pages," he continued coldly, with another one of his keen, paralyzing glances.

Maddie's heart sank but immediately lifted again. After all, what was one thirty-page paper compared to being kicked out of school? She almost laughed, but she kept her face composed. "I understand," she said in a serious tone.

He looked at her appraisingly for a moment. "If this paper is *excellent,* and if you merit an A on the final exam, I will give you a C for the class." He turned away abruptly and reopened the heavy book he had been reading when she came in. "Needless to say, your continued presence at this school still remains very much at risk. You will have to prove yourself at every turn."

"I understand."

There was no response. Professor Harrison was looking pointedly at the book on his desk, and Maddie realized she had been dismissed. The old intimidating scholar was back, but Maddie still felt like jumping up and kissing him. But there was no point in skating out onto thin ice again!

Carefully holding her elation in check, she rose to her feet. It felt like a lifetime had passed since she first sat down. Walking swiftly to the door, she paused with hand on the knob and looked back. "Thank you," she said simply.

Professor Harrison made a slight, dismissing movement with his hand. Maddie smiled and stepped out into the hallway again, closing the door behind her.

As she walked down the steps of the faculty office building, Maddie drank in deep gulps of fresh air, feeling renewed. Her miracle had happened after all, she thought joyously. Not that it hadn't meant taking a trip through fire, but ultimately it *had* worked out!

And as she thought about the paper she had to undertake, Stu's face immediately sprang to mind, and she smiled with relief. She couldn't wait to tell him what she had done and apologize for being such an idiot. Losing him had seemed like a good way to punish herself for betraying Sam, but she didn't need to do that anymore.

Then, as quickly as it had appeared, Maddie's smile faded from her face, and she stopped dead in her tracks. The worst wasn't over yet. There was still Sam to face.

Maddie glanced at her watch as she climbed the stairs to the second floor of Rogers House. Well over an hour had gone by since she had left Sam at the Dixie Diner. Knowing Sam, and Sam's relationship with Stacy and Roni, Maddie was sure that Sam had gone home immediately, seeking the warmth and reassurance of her friends.

She stepped onto the landing and squared her shoulders. This was something she had to go through with, and delaying would only make it worse. She strode down the hallway and opened the door of suite 2C.

Sitting by the window, Roni looked up with a stony face as Maddie came into the living room. Stacy turned around on the couch, and her blue eyes gave Maddie a cold, hard look. Obviously, they knew. Maddie almost lost her nerve as she read the bitter anger and disappointment in their expressions, but she turned to close the door carefully and then faced them again.

"I've spoken to Professor Harrison," she said

quietly, standing rigidly straight and looking at the floor. "Sam won't be getting into any trouble."

There was a caustic silence; Maddie thought she heard a tiny sigh of relief escape from Stacy. Her eyes went swiftly to the closed door of Stacy and Sam's room. She hoped Sam wouldn't come out. Not quite yet, she begged silently. She needed to recover from facing Roni and Stacy before she could bear to speak to Sam. Taking another breath, Maddie said, "I'll go pack. I'll be out of here as soon as I can."

Her hard-won composure lasted just long enough to get into her room and shut the door. But then the tears began slipping relentlessly down Maddie's cheeks. In such a short time she had made three very special friendships. And in just as short a time, she had destroyed them.

She looked with blurred eyes around the room she shared with Roni. On her bed was the little teddy bear Stacy had given her on the day she had moved in. All at once, that was too much to bear, and Maddie dropped down onto her bed, sobbing as quietly as she could into the stuffed animal's fur. She pressed her knuckles to her teeth and squeezed her eyes shut hard enough to make them hurt.

After a few minutes of aching tears, she forced herself to stop crying and stood up, firmly wiping her face with the back of her hand. She crossed to the closet and began methodically taking her clothes off their hangers and tossing them onto the bed. Her bureau was next, and one after the other, she emptied the drawers.

She faltered on the brink of tears again as she pulled out the black sweater she'd bought in Atlanta. But she just sighed loudly and threw it onto the pile. There was no sense in being nostalgic. She owed it to her suitemates to clear out as soon as she could so they didn't have to have her around anymore.

She dragged her two suitcases from under the bed and began filling them. Sniffing quietly, she fastened the straps of one and shut it. Then, behind her, she heard the door open.

Maddie stiffened, and her hands stopped in mid-air. Apprehensively, she turned around to see Roni sitting down at her desk. Roni began fiddling nervously with the switch of the desk lamp, turning it on and off, on and off.

"You're packing," Roni observed, her voice sounding more like a feeble croak.

Maddie's eyes went back to her suitcases, and she set her mouth in a bitter line. "Yes."

"Are you being kicked out?"

With difficulty, Maddie swallowed and shook her head. "No. Professor Harrison said he wouldn't take it to the honor board."

Roni whistled quietly. "You're lucky."

There was a long pause, during which Roni still twiddled the light switch, obviously considering saying something. "You know, I smashed up Stacy's car a few weeks ago. She only got it fixed a few days before you moved in."

Tired, unhappy, and uncertain what this was leading to, Maddie sat down slowly on the edge of her bed. "So?" she prompted, her voice hesitant.

A quick blush colored Roni's cheeks.

"Roni, what? What does that have to do with anything?"

Roni pushed her chair back, scraping it along the floor, and turned to look Maddie in the eyes. "Look, I don't pretend to understand how you could actually have copied Sam's paper. But I know what it feels like to be in a corner, and what it's like to know you let your friends down."

Maddie's chin quivered, and she put a hand up to her mouth.

"It's like you just wish none of it ever happened, and you're paralyzed," Roni went on, squeezing her hands between her knees. She looked up again, and her normally laughing green eyes pleaded desperately with Maddie. "Is *that* what happened?"

Pressing both hands over her mouth, Maddie nodded, feeling the tears spill out over her hot cheeks as she met Roni's eyes.

Roni was crying, too. "Maddie, Sam really likes you, you know! She really thinks you're a special person."

Maddie turned away. "What are you trying to tell me, Roni?" she choked out miserably.

"All I'm trying to say, is that—I thought Stacy would hate me forever. I really did. Maddie, I was blind drunk, I didn't even know where I was! And I totaled her car." Maddie heard Roni draw a deep, shuddery breath. "She was really upset, but I mean, she understood—and she eventually forgave me."

"It's not the same," Maddie whispered, staring blindly at her open suitcase. She shook her head hopelessly. "It's not the same. Sam could never forgive me for this."

"Even if she doesn't, I think you should go talk to her."

Maddie nodded and wiped away a tear. "I know. I have to."

Quickly, Roni crossed the room and took Maddie by the arm. "Do it now, Maddie," she said urgently, her eyes searching Maddie's face. "Do it now."

For a long, tense moment the two girls stood locked together. Maddie stared down at Roni's hand gripping her wrist and nodded slowly. "Okay."

With that she turned and opened the door to the living room. Stacy looked up briefly, and her eyes darted past Maddie to Roni. Then she lowered her head again.

Maddie kept her eyes fixed on the door across the room and walked to it mechanically. Her feet felt like lead. "Sam?" she called softly, rapping timidly on the door. "Sam, it's me. Maddie."

Painful seconds ticked by before Sam answered, and when she did her voice was barely audible. "Come in."

Maddie threw a last, anxious glance over her shoulder: Roni and Stacy were watching her intently. Then she turned the knob and went in.

Sam was sitting at her desk, carefully filing loose papers in a notebook. Her back was to Maddie, and she didn't turn around. Instead, she picked up a hole punch and began making holes in some photocopies.

Watching her, Maddie was filled with sadness and longing. What they had—what they used to have—had been the makings of a really special, once-in-a-lifetime relationship. She had always felt closer to Sam than to the others. Maybe it was their common background, or the fact that Sam had recognized and reached out to a lonely Maddie in Daytona Beach. Whatever that special something was, it had drawn them very close in a very short time. And Maddie knew that up until that point, she hadn't realized what a priceless thing she had destroyed.

"Oh, Sam," she said, her voice catching in her throat. "I was such a jerk. And I'm so, so sorry." She could see Sam's hands trembling as she aligned another few pages with a sheet of loose-leaf. "I—I know you probably hate me now, and you never want to see me—or, or talk to me again. But I had to tell you that you won't be getting into trouble. I know I waited too long, but I did take care of it. I'm really sorry you had to suffer for a whole week."

Sam lowered her head slightly, but she still didn't turn around. Her shoulders twitched once, as though she were fighting hard to keep herself under control. Maddie's heart ached at Sam's silent reproach, and she turned to leave. There didn't seem to be anything left to say.

As her hand touched the doorknob, she heard Sam clear her throat. "How could you *do* it?" Sam asked, her voice thick with emotion.

Maddie shook her head helplessly, and Sam finally turned to look at her with tortured eyes. "I don't know," Maddie whispered. "I just don't know—I was so desperate. I never thought there would be a time when I wouldn't be able to do my work—I always have, it always seemed so easy and automatic. But I was wrong. I just tried to do too much and I . . ." She trailed off, shaking her head again at the futility of an explanation.

Sam suddenly looked away. "What are they going to do to you?"

"Professor Harrison said he'll pass me if I turn in a special assignment. He isn't going to report this incident to the honor board, he said." Maddie sighed wearily. The relief at her professor's verdict had disappeared, leaving only an empty, lonely sadness in its place.

"You mean, you don't have to leave? You get to stay here?"

Maddie caught her breath at the angry, shocked tone of Sam's words. She stared hard at the floor, willing herself not to cry again. "Not Hawthorne. But I'm moving back to my aunt's house right away."

There was a strangled whimper from Sam, and Maddie looked up to see her shaking her head, tears streaming down her face. "No, Maddie, don't!" she cried, rising to her feet.

Amazed, Maddie watched as Sam took a few steps toward her. "What?" she gasped.

Sam shook her head, her face contorted with grief. "I don't want you to leave, Maddie! I should hate you, but I can't! I don't want to lose you as a friend." Before Maddie realized what was happening, Sam was holding her tight, crying into her shoulder. "I don't want you to leave!"

For a moment, Maddie was too stunned to respond. Sam still liked her, and she might forgive her! A heart-wrenching sob welled up in Maddie's throat, and she hugged Sam back fiercely. "Oh, Sam, I'm so sorry, I'm so sorry!" she cried, burying her face in Sam's hair. "I'm so sorry!"

Behind them, the door opened. "Great! Now I've seen just about everything!" Roni exclaimed.

Chapter 14

Maddie and Sam broke apart, both wiping their eyes and sniffing loudly. Maddie, for one, felt as if she had just weathered a terrible storm, and that now the clouds were finally breaking up. Roni was sitting on the edge of Stacy's bed, shaking her head.

"What am I going to do with you two?" she drawled, and rolled her eyes.

"What's going on in here?" asked Stacy, poking her head in through the half-open door. She quickly took in the scene and raised her eyebrows in surprise.

Sam laughed weakly. "That's right. We decided to kiss and make up."

Maddie's knees suddenly felt like rubber, and she lowered herself quickly into the chair at Sam's desk. Involuntary shivers kept racking her body as the tension of the last week was finally released. Slowly she raised her eyes to Sam's face, to reassure herself that she was really and truly forgiven. Sam gave her a quirky half smile and shrugged, as if to say "What else could I do?"

"Well-l-l!" Stacy let out a huge sigh of relief and glanced at Maddie.

Instinctively, Maddie knew they shouldn't discuss it anymore right now. All might be forgiven, but the wounds were still fresh and tender. Maybe later they would be able to talk about it without feeling awkward, but for the time being, better let well enough alone.

"But, uh, Maddie?" Roni said tentatively, tucking her knees up under her on the bed. "What are you going to tell your parents?"

Maddie's head reeled. Biting her lip, Maddie fidgeted with the hole punch Sam had left on the desk and squeezed it compulsively. That was something she had put firmly out of her mind at first—but now it had to be faced.

"I think," she began slowly, drawing her eyebrows together in concentration. "I think I'll cross that bridge when I come to it—when I get home at the end of the semester."

Looking up, she met looks of skepticism from her suitemates, and she shook her head decisively. "I've been needing an excuse to talk to them about academic pressure for a long time, and I guess this has really brought it to a head. They're going to flip when I turn up with a C for Shakespeare, but they'll just have to understand that I'm not superhuman. I can't be—and I don't *want* to be, either," she added vehemently.

"You—you don't think they'll make you move off campus, do you?" Sam asked with a worried frown. "They didn't really want you to be in here in the first place."

Maddie grimaced. "That'll probably be their first reaction. But I'll just refuse, that's all," she went on, lifting her chin defiantly. "There is such a thing as a happy medium, you know, and I'm going to make them understand that. I *know* I can live on campus, have a normal social life, and still do well in school."

There was a silence, and Maddie's thoughts raced ahead to the inevitable ugly confrontation with her folks. But she had to make them understand her. All her life she had agreed to follow their lead, but it was time for her to make her own decisions about how she lived her life. She knew it wasn't fair to blame them for what she had done—but they had always encouraged her to study instead of play, and she had never fought it. So, looking back, it was no surprise that at her first chance, she had gone racing off wildly in every direction to make up for lost time.

She drew a deep breath as her confidence and hope grew. It would be rough, but somehow she'd make them understand. When she got home in May, it would definitely be the right time to talk it out with them.

"Maddie, what kind of deal did the professor make with you?" Stacy asked, looking at her curiously. She leaned back on the bed and propped her head up with one hand.

"A special assignment—well, a superlong paper," Maddie said, not wanting to get into all the details right away. "It has to do with staging a play."

Sam chuckled softly. "I know someone who might be able to help with *that.*"

Maddie lifted her eyebrows inquisitively, then realized that Sam was talking about Stu. Her throat tightened again as she pictured his face; she could almost see him tossing his bangs out of his eyes. She owed him an explanation for her bizarre behavior, if nothing else. But she seriously doubted they could even be friends after she told him. Her face clouded with worry.

"I don't know," she muttered. "I've acted like a total jerk around him lately."

Roni let out a groan. "Maddie, don't you know that that's par for the course? Every girl in the world acts like a total jerk around her boyfriend once in a while. It's just one of those things you have to get through."

"He's not my boyfriend!" Maddie corrected her, a blush coloring her cheeks.

The other three looked at one another. Then Stacy laughed, shaking her head at the ceiling. "Sure, Maddie."

Her blush deepened. "He isn't, really. We—I mean, he and I—"

"Madison Lerner." Roni heaved a sigh of weary patience and waggled a finger at Maddie. "Just go talk to him. Go for it. You're on a roll."

Maddie smiled ruefully. "I guess this is my day for confessions, huh?"

From the corner of her eye, she noticed Sam pick up the hole punch again and fiddle with it. It might be her imagination, but Maddie suspected Sam was beginning to feel uncomfortable talking about what had just happened. Some hard feelings were still there, hidden just under the surface. Maddie figured it was probably a good time to leave and let things cool off for a while in suite 2C.

"Okay," she said briskly, rising to her feet with a brave smile. "I will. But I sure don't know what to say to him. Last time I saw him, I was a complete idiot. I just hope he can understand."

Sam spoke up softly. "Just tell him the truth, Maddie. He'll probably understand."

They stared at one another for a moment. Then Maddie nodded quickly and left the room.

Stu lived in one of the newer dorms at the other end of campus, and Maddie ran along the path by the lake with a fluttering heart. She had stopped by his room once before a movie, and now she retraced her steps up to the fourth floor. Taking a deep breath, she rapped on the door.

His roommate answered her knock, and he registered a look of surprise as he recognized her. "Hi—uh, you're looking for Stu?"

She nodded, and her eyes darted past him into the room. There was no sign of Stu.

"He's not here—he's at the theater, I think."

Maddie rolled her eyes at her own stupidity. "Of course he is," she groaned, smacking her forehead with one palm. "I'm kind of slow on the uptake today."

"No problem." He laughed.

Within minutes Maddie was flying across the Hawthorne campus again, this time in the direction of the Fine Arts Complex. The familiar, musty smell of the theater greeted her as she took the carpeted steps two at a time, and her hopes soared. She couldn't wait to see Stu, even though she couldn't be certain whether he would listen to her. Or, if he did listen, whether he would ever speak to her again.

When she opened the auditorium doors, she spotted him immediately because all the house lights were on. He was sitting about halfway up the aisle, with his long legs propped up on the seat in front of him. He was studying a clipboard in his hands, while up onstage, the cast of *A Midsummer Night's Dream* blocked out the first scene of act two.

She approached slowly, trying to form the right words in her head. But all she could think of was how nice and reassuring he looked sitting there with his legs up on the seat. Holding her breath, she slipped onto the seat behind him.

"Hi."

Stu jumped in his seat and pulled his legs down so he could scramble around to see her. Surprise, hope, wariness—a whole range of emotions passed across his features as their eyes met. "Hi yourself," he said finally.

"Can we talk for a minute?"

He lowered his eyes, then looked up again.

"Sure. Let's go into the office." Without checking to see if she was following him, he strode down the aisle and up the short flight of steps to the backstage door. They passed through the dark hallway crowded with scenery and furniture, and Stu opened the office door. Maddie sat on the edge of a chair, and Stu perched on the desk, looking inquiringly at her.

"I wanted to apologize for acting so childish," Maddie began at once, fixing her eyes on his. "I never should have said those things to you. I didn't mean them." He made a dismissive motion with one hand, and she went on, "But I want to tell you what I did—why I was acting so crazy."

"You don't have to if you don't want to, Maddie. Really." His old smile was back, and he shook his head. "I'm just glad . . . well, you know."

"No, wait a minute," she went on breathlessly. The look in his warm green eyes made her heart pound wildly, but she felt that she had to let him know what she had done. He was ready to forgive her for being so rude—but would he forgive her for everything? She stood up and began pacing the tiny office. Stu followed her with his eyes.

"When I moved onto campus, I guess I took on more than I could handle, and I got myself into a big mess," she said, speaking rapidly, almost to herself. "You kept asking me if I was getting my paper done, and I lied to you."

She turned to look at him briefly and saw a puzzled frown on his face. "To make a long story short, I ended up copying Sam's paper," she blurted, and bit her lip. His frown turned to astonishment and incredulity.

"I thought I could get away with it—but that's not what happened," she went on in a rush, pacing again with her arms folded across her chest. "I felt terrible—I felt awful! But, well, anyway the professor found out about it, and everything hit the fan. I just went sort of—haywire, I guess."

She paused and stared at the floor. She was afraid to meet his eyes.

"What happened?" he said quietly.

With a little shake of her head, Maddie sighed. "Well, I told Sam—she was being accused of cheating, too, and didn't know who it was. She thought she was going to be expelled! And then I went and confessed to Professor Harrison, and . . ." She paused to catch her breath and stole a glance at Stu. He was frowning at the floor. "And anyway," she continued wearily, "I have to do a paper about staging techniques for this play, and then he might just pass me."

Stu nodded thoughtfully but didn't look up. He seemed pretty upset. Maddie gulped. "I thought I should just warn you that I'll probably be hanging around here to watch a lot of the time. I'm sorry if I seem like I'm in the way."

At that he looked up with a keen, penetrating glance that shot right through her heart. "I can't believe you did that," he said in an incredulous voice.

She looked away quickly. "I know. Believe me, I've asked myself a hundred times how I could have done it. Especially to Sam! And I know perfectly well it was a rotten, lousy, despicable, horrible thing to do."

Amazingly, Stu laughed. "No, not that." She whirled around, and he gave her a faint smile. "Believe me, it's easy enough to understand how anybody in this place could do something crazy. There's a lot of pressure. It's not all that hard to believe that even someone like you could do it."

She shook her head uncomprehendingly. "Huh?"

"No—what I can't believe is that you turned yourself in," he went on, coming close to her and taking her hands. "I don't know that many people who would. I don't know if I would," he added truthfully. She stared up into his eyes in speechless wonder. "I think it was a really brave thing to do."

"Then—then you don't . . . ?"

In answer, he reached out and took her hands, pulling her toward him. With a grateful sigh of relief, Maddie leaned into him and rested her head on his chest. His arms tightened around her, and she could feel his cheek rubbing against her hair.

"I can't believe this is happening," she murmured dreamily. She opened her eyes and got a close-up view of his red polo shirt. Leaning back, she looked up into his face. "I can't believe you don't think I'm the most horrible person in the world."

A wicked smile twitched at the corners of his mouth as he returned her gaze. "Just remind me not to leave my Greek history paper lying around where you can get your hands on it."

"Oh—you!" With a laughing gasp, Maddie pulled

away and raised her hand as if to hit him, but he grabbed her wrists and pulled her back to him.

"Seriously, Maddie. I really like you. I did from the beginning. You can always talk to me—if you ever get yourself into a mess again, I'd do anything I could to help you out, you know that."

She didn't say anything, and he leaned back for a moment to look gravely into her eyes. "You do know that, don't you?"

A smile broke slowly across her face, and she nodded. "I guess I do now."

"Maddie! What happened?"

After she shut the door of the suite behind her, Maddie turned to look at Roni with a sheepish grin. "He said he understood," she said, shaking her head with wonder at the memory. She crossed the living room and slowly sank onto the couch next to Roni, lost in thought. "I can't believe this all worked out. It should have been impossible, but you actually forgive me." Turning quickly, she looked into Roni's eyes. "You *really* do? I mean, you should really be so disgusted with me. I would be."

Roni leaned forward, looking completely serious and sincere for once. "Listen," she said, putting a hand on Maddie's knee, "someone once told me that you shouldn't come down on people too hard unless you're totally sure you'd never do what they did in a million years."

"People in glass houses shouldn't throw stones?" Maddie suggested with a sorry grin. She poked her foot at a magazine lying facedown on the floor and sighed wearily.

Roni shrugged. "Something like that, I guess. Anyway, so far this year, we've all pulled some pretty bizarre stunts." She smiled a faint, reminiscent smile, her eyes downcast. "Believe me, I've learned a lot more at college than I expected to, but none of it in class!"

"Oh, Roni, get out of here!"

They laughed, and both leaned back against the couch, staring at the ceiling in silence for a few moments. Sam and Stacy found them like that when they returned from the laundry room minutes later. Maddie rolled her head to one side on the back of the couch to gape at them. "You guys just did *laundry?*"

Stacy put a bottle of fabric softener down on the table and shot Maddie a lofty glance. "Life goes on, my dear. Life goes on."

As Roni snorted with laughter, Sam crossed over to the couch and sat in the chair next to Maddie. "How did it go with Stu?" she asked quietly.

"Everything's fine," Maddie replied with a warm smile. "I'll never understand it, but everything's fine."

"Speaking of everything being fine," Roni piped up suddenly. "Did anyone happen to notice what was on the menu for dinner tonight?" As the others looked at her blankly, she grimaced. "Everything with dinner is definitely *not* fine. Tuna casserole."

"Not again!" Sam complained, closing her eyes in an agony of despair.

"Yes indeed," Roni breezed on. "And therefore I propose we put into practice the techniques of primitive societies, and go hunting and gathering."

"Maybe we could find a nice lawn and just graze," Stacy drawled, squeezing in on the couch and kicking off her sandals.

Maddie beamed at her suitemates. "How about I take us all out to DelRio's, huh? My treat?"

The others exchanged a fleeting glance. Sam shook her head uncertainly. "I don't know, Maddie. Are you sure you shouldn't—"

"Stay home and study?" Roni and Stacy chimed in together.

Trying hard not to laugh, Maddie pulled a pillow out from behind her back and brought it down on Roni's head. "Take that, you swine! We're going and that's final. And," she added, smiling serenely at the others, "we'll make it an early night."

Sam grinned. "It's a deal. Let's go."

Here's a sneak preview of *Final Exams*, book number six in the continuing *ROOMMATES* series.

An hour later, Maddie had taken a relaxing bubble bath and climbed into bed, her Western Civilization textbook in hand. She tried reading a few pages, but her eyes kept closing and finally she drifted off. It was a light sleep, though, and Maddie was aware of talking in the living room and the smell of popcorn wafting through the suite. In a little while, she heard Roni come in, shuck off her clothes' and get to bed.

Maddie didn't want Roni to know she was awake, so she lay with her eyes open, facing away from her roommate. She didn't want to risk any unpleasant conversation.

Roni began snoring, obviously in a deep sleep, but there was no way Maddie could get back to that state. She twisted and turned. First she heard Sam come in, and then Stacy. Finally the suite was dark and quiet. Maddie smoothed her pillowcase, hoping it would be for the final time, and that sleep would now come. She closed her eyes tightly. Her lids were finally getting heavier when suddenly she smelled something. Go back to sleep, she moaned silently to herself. It's probably from another apartment.

But as the seconds ticked by, the acrid odor seemed to be getting heavier instead of going away. Maddie sat up. Her heart beat a little faster, until a picture of Stacy sitting in the dark and smoking a cigarette flashed into her mind. Stacy had done that before, she remembered. Once more Maddie settled under the covers. Her eyes were growing heavier, but as much as she wanted to give in to sleep, a part of her noticed that the smell still lingered. Get up, she told herself. You won't be able to sleep until you check.

Maddie moved softly from her bed and padded over to the door. She opened it a crack, but instead of seeing Stacy on the couch, cigarette in hand, Maddie gazed in horror at the heart-stopping sight of a bright flame climbing up the side of the curtain.

Maddie shoved her fist in her mouth to stifle the shriek that was climbing in her throat. If she started screaming now, she might never stop, she was certain of that. Forcing herself to think calmly, she looked around the room. Should she try to put out the fire herself? How could she? Then her eyes focused on Roni's sleeping form. She had to get Roni out of the suite.

Maddie ran over to her roommate and began shaking her, hard. "Get up, Roni. Get up."

Roni rolled over and opened one eye. "What is it, Maddie? Bad dream?" she asked sarcastically.

"There's a fire in the living room," Maddie answered, trying to keep her terror under control.

"What?" Roni bolted upright.

Maddie tugged at her arm. "Come on, you've got to get out of here. Just leave. I'm going to wake Stacy and Sam."

"Not alone," Roni said, her voice shaking. "I'm going with you."

"All right, but let's soak some towels and put them over our faces. We're going to need them so we don't inhale too much smoke. The fire's still on the window wall," Maddie yelled, "but it's crawling along the baseboard toward Sam and Stacy's room!"

"How can you see anything?" Roni asked, her voice muffled by the wet towel. "The smoke is so thick!"

"And it's getting thicker!" Maddie yelled back. "Let's get a move on, but be careful."